"Don't look at me like that," he said curtly.

She veiled her eyes with her lashes. "Why not?"

"Because when you look at me like that I want to kiss you. And if I kiss you again, I may not be able to stop." His expression seemed forbidding in the semi-darkness, but she thought she could detect a trace of self-mockery in the clipped words.

"I . . . didn't ask you to stop," she said huskily. "Don't you find me . . . desirable?"

"You know damn well I find you desirable." He pulled her angrily against his thighs. "You know what you're doing to me; you can feel it. But I'm too old to enjoy sneaking casual kisses on a dance floor, Amie."

She reached up and touched her hand to his mouth. "Kiss me," she whispered.

"I must be crazy to do this." His words were a shaky murmur against her lips, and she could feel the roar of her own blood pounding in her ears as Liam's mouth trailed a burning path of kisses from her throat to her lips. She needed no persuasion . . .

Dear Reader:

As the months go by, we continue to receive word from you that SECOND CHANCE AT LOVE romances are providing you with the kind of romantic entertainment you're looking for. In your letters you've voiced enthusiastic support for SECOND CHANCE AT LOVE, you've shared your thoughts on how personally meaningful the books are, and you've suggested ideas and changes for future books. Although we can't always reply to your letters as quickly as we'd like, please be assured that we appreciate your comments. Your thoughts are all-important to us!

We're glad many of you have come to associate SECOND CHANCE AT LOVE books with our butterfly trademark. We think the butterfly is a perfect symbol of the reaffirmation of life and thrilling new love that SECOND CHANCE AT LOVE heroines and heroes find together in each story. We hope you keep asking for the "butterfly books," and that, when you buy one—whether by a favorite author or a talented new writer—you're sure of a good read. You can trust all SECOND CHANCE AT LOVE books to live up to the high standards of romantic fiction you've come to expect.

So happy reading, and keep your letters coming!

With warm wishes,

Ellen Edwards

Ellen Edwards
SECOND CHANCE AT LOVE
The Berkley/Jove Publishing Group
200 Madison Avenue
New York, NY 10016

IMPRISONED HEART
JASMINE CRAIG

SECOND CHANCE AT LOVE
BOOK

Second Chance at Love books are published by
The Berkley/Jove Publishing Group
200 Madison Avenue, New York, NY 10016

CHAPTER ONE

THE PERSONNEL MANAGER stood up, smiling politely to indicate that the interview was over. "I wish you every success, Amie," he said. "I'm sure our new president will accept my recommendation and offer you the job."

Amie hesitated for only a second or two before returning Mr. Hubert's handshake. "Thank you," she said, her quiet voice sounding cool and efficient. "I'll do my best to live up to your expectations."

"Good, good. Well, the president is waiting to interview you, so why don't you go straight up to his office. You know where it is?"

"Yes," she said. "The corner suite on the twentieth floor. Mr. Hubert, I'm not sure that I want—"

"Don't worry, Amie. The reports I had from your current boss were excellent. I'd never have recommended

you for the position if I didn't think you were the best
secretary in the company."

"Thank you," she said, managing to keep her expression as cool and self-assured as before. She had been
hiding the truth about herself for four years now, and
her face was no longer the open mirror of all her feelings
it once had been. She erased a tiny frown from her forehead as she left Mr. Hubert's office, not allowing herself
to reveal any of the tumultuous thoughts churning inside
her head. Half an hour ago she had been no more than
a secretary in the sales department, a humble cog safely
lost in the vastness of the National Development Corporation. Now she was being considered for the job of
personal assistant to the president of the company. It was
a promotional leap greater than anything she had dreamed
of achieving.

The full implications of the change suddenly struck
her with chilling force, and she stopped in her tracks,
turning around and hurrying back to Mr. Hubert's office.
She was on the point of knocking at his door when her
hand hesitated, poised only inches away from the frosted
glass panels. What excuse could she give for refusing
the promotion? She couldn't say she'd learned to feel
safe, almost invisible, in her humdrum job in the sales
department. She couldn't say she didn't want to accept
a job that carried real responsibility and a great deal of
visibility within the company.

She fought to overcome the cowardly urge to knock
on Mr. Hubert's door. The past was over, she reminded
herself. It was time she forgot something that had happened four years ago in a small town miles away from
Chicago. Her hand fell back to her side, and she walked
quickly away before she could lose her courage again.

Her classic features still betrayed no sign of her inner
turmoil. She had learned the hard way how to keep her
emotions hidden, and nowadays her dark blue eyes rarely
expressed any stronger feeling than polite interest or mild
boredom.

It was at moments like this that she realized the trau-
mas of the past weren't completely behind her. She still
felt guilty every time she was promoted. In some secret
part of her soul she believed herself to be unworthy, as
if no amount of hard work or superior efficiency could
ever entitle her to success. Even after four years of an-
onymity in a big city, memories from her trial still haunted
her dreams.

Determinedly she pushed the intrusive images from
the past to the back of her mind and began to make her
way across the crowded main office. The huge room was
noisier than usual as groups of chattering typists returned
from their lunch break. Amie scarcely noticed the babble
of voices around her. Gossip had become a fact of company life over the past couple of weeks. The rumor mills
had been grinding overtime ever since a terse announce-
ment had heralded the appointment of Liam Kane as
National's new president.

With the prospect of a job interview looming ahead,
Amie tried to recall everything she had heard about Mr.
Kane. She wished she'd paid more attention to the rumors. The office grapevine, more efficient than any high-
tech surveillance system, had reported that he was a
financial wizard, an acclaimed troubleshooter, hired away
from the federal government with explicit orders to pull
National back into sound economic health.

As far as his personal life was concerned, the information had been less precise though no less voluminous.

Amie knew only that Liam Kane was supposed to be devastatingly attractive, utterly ruthless, and not yet forty years old. His personal charisma was fast becoming accepted as a fact rather than mere gossip, since every female employee privileged to meet him returned dreamy-eyed from the encounter. Moreover, Beth Mittel, the acknowledged source of all the hottest snippets of gossip, asserted that Kane had dined out each night with a different vice-president—and a different beautiful woman as his companion.

His ruthlessness was not yet considered similarly proven, although rumors of imminent firings circulated constantly and two elderly division managers were known to have been eased into retirement.

Nevertheless, Amie thought Liam Kane would be an interesting man to work for, and fortunately she knew herself to be entirely indifferent to his personal charms. She was in no danger of falling victim to his much-vaunted sex appeal. Her one reckless plunge into love had been disastrous enough to give her lifetime immunity to masculine charm.

She slipped into the ladies' room and checked that no stray wisps of hair had escaped from the severity of her tightly coiled braids. She wanted to impress Liam Kane, she decided suddenly, because she wanted this job. After four years of isolation, four years of being afraid to make friends, it was time to break out and make contact with the world. The position as personal assistant to the president would offer her the fresh start she needed.

Her oval face looked pale under the harsh fluorescent lights, and her ash-blond hair underlined the impression of remoteness. Her mouth was taut, the softness of her lips tightly controlled. She took off her glasses and cleaned the tinted lenses with a tissue, then stared with unusual intensity into the mirror. Without the concealing lenses, her eyes gleamed with a sapphire sheen, and her face seemed to blur into an unfamiliar vulnerability. Hastily she pushed the glasses back into place, so that the shadowed lenses screened out all traces of emotion. Her face was once again the safe, blank mask she had learned to hide behind. She reminded herself that Mr. Hubert had recommended her for this job precisely because she was efficient and didn't allow emotions to get in the way of her work. This was hardly an appropriate moment to start a reappraisal of her whole attitude toward life.

Her feelings were back under their usual tight control by the time the elevator halted on the twentieth floor. The door to the president's suite of offices stood open, but there was no sign of a secretary in the outer office. Amie walked into the empty room, the sound of her footsteps deadened by the thick carpet. Hesitantly she tapped on the heavy walnut door leading to the inner office, but it remained firmly closed.

She waited for a moment or two, hoping Mr. Kane's secretary would return; but as far as she could see, the twentieth floor was devoid of people. A faint murmur of voices finally became audible from the president's inner office, and with a tiny shrug Amie knocked loudly on the glowing walnut panels of the door.

"Come in!"

She obeyed the muffled command and walked into the spacious presidential office. Liam Kane stood at his desk, his back to her as he spoke rapidly into the telephone. There was nobody else in the room. He finished his phone conversation with a final crisp instruction and immediately turned around, loosening his tie and unfastening the top button of his shirt as his gaze ran over her in a swift, comprehensive appraisal.

Amie stopped dead in her tracks. Her body felt as if it had been flash-frozen into numbness. Only the accelerated rhythm of her heart, racing with fear, reminded her that she was still very much alive. She stared at the corded muscles of his neck and at the pulse she could just glimpse beating beneath the knot of his tie, and then, with a phenomenal effort of will, she managed to lift her gaze so that it was level with his.

His tawny eyes stared back at her from a face that was more tanned than she remembered, but she noticed few other changes. He still projected an aura of controlled power and explosive energy held on the shortest of leashes. She wanted to turn away, but as always when he looked at her, she found even a small movement of her head impossible. She stood shivering, but incapable of protest, while he silently assessed the changes wrought by the last four years. She strove to keep her expression uncaring, knowing that her efforts were almost certainly doomed to failure. He could undoubtedly gauge the turbulent state of her feelings with the absolute precision instilled by his training as a professional investigator.

He came from behind the desk and started to walk across the room. She held her breath, bracing herself to meet the onslaught of his scorn. When he was quite close to her, he stopped and held out his hand. To her astonishment, she saw that he was smiling, a warm smile of devastating charm.

"Hello," he said. "I'm Liam Kane and you must be Amie Fletcher." The firm touch of his handshake sent a paralyzing ripple of fear snaking up her arm, but he let go of her hand and moved casually away as if he were unaware of her violent reaction. He smiled at her again. "The personnel manager told me you'd be coming right up. He gave you such a glowing report that I've been looking forward to meeting you. Finding a competent secretary is usually such a nuisance. Did Mr. Hubert give you any precise idea of what working for me will entail?"

This must be his idea of a cruel joke, she thought wildly. It was some perverted form of punishment he'd decided to inflict on her because the jury had acquitted her. She ran her tongue over dry lips. Her throat felt so constricted that she was surprised when she heard herself speaking. "Mr. Hubert warned me that you wouldn't be keeping strictly to office hours," she said, answering his question because her brain was incapable of formulating a question of its own.

"Will that cause problems, Ms. Fletcher? Do you have personal commitments that make it necessary for you to leave work promptly at five?"

"No I don't, Mr. Kane." She wondered if he could see her heart pounding against her rib cage. Surely he could see that the palms of her hands were damp with nervous tension. She finally managed to tear her gaze away from the hypnotic power of his eyes and stared fixedly at a hairline crack in the wall behind his left shoulder.

"Let me tell you how I like to organize my work with my secretary, so that you can get some idea of whether or not you'd enjoy the job. First of all, I need somebody who can take total charge of the details of administering an office. I've been with the company less than two weeks, but I can see I'm going to be doing a great deal of traveling. I don't want to find myself scheduled in two places at once, and I want to have absolute confidence when I'm away that my secretary has all routine matters under control. I also need an assistant who can differentiate between a routine problem and a major crisis."

"I make the travel arrangements for most of the reps in the sales department," Amie said. "Sometimes their calendars can become pretty complicated. I think the salesmen have found me reliable." Perhaps if she didn't look at him again she would manage to get out of his office without making a complete fool of herself. But why, in heaven's name, was he pretending he didn't recognize her?

"Good. In addition, I expect my secretary to respond to routine correspondence on her own. On the other hand, I dictate complicated letters into a tape recorder, so you won't need shorthand to work with me. Mr. Hubert told me your typing is excellent, and you've had some experience working with computers?"

Whatever color was left in her cheeks drained away as he spoke. "Yes," she said, hating him and fearing him in almost equal proportions. "I've had more experience working with computers than most secretaries."

"And Mr. Hubert tells me you can even spell!" Liam Kane's voice deepened with a hint of laughter. "With so many outstanding qualifications, I can't imagine how you've managed to hide in the regional sales department for so long. I think Mr. Hubert said you've been working at National for nearly four years?"

Hate won out over fear. Damn him, whatever cruel game he was playing! She wouldn't allow him to see how successful his subtle form of torture was. With superhuman effort she kept every trace of panic out of her voice. "Yes, Mr. Kane," she said bleakly. "In October

I'll have been here four years."

"Then I'll be able to rely on you to fill me in on the names and faces of the people around the home office. I rarely forget a face, but I'm cursed with a terrible memory for names."

"How unfortunate, Mr. Kane," she said, and felt her hands curl into claws around her notebook. Is that why you've changed *your* name? she wanted to scream at him. Have you already forgotten that four years ago you called yourself Lawrence King? Is your memory for names *that* bad?

"There is one problem we should discuss," he said.

Now, she thought with a flash of near-hysterical relief. Now he was going to talk about what had happened. Now he was going to accuse her of being a thief. Perversely, she wished suddenly that he would keep the game going on just a little longer. There was a strange, masochistic satisfaction in talking so politely to the man who had shattered every one of her youthful dreams. It was like probing a wound to see if it would bleed. At least the pain served as a reminder that she was still alive.

"What precisely is the problem you mentioned, Mr. Kane?" She was shaking inside, but her voice was low and calm. She wouldn't give him the satisfaction of letting him see how his questions terrified her.

"It's my handwriting," he said with a cheerful grin. "I try to avoid bombarding my staff with memos, but when I can't help writing one, or when I have to prepare a report, I tend to scribble out the rough draft in an abominable, illegible handwriting. Plane journeys seem to have a particularly disastrous effect on me. I'm inspired by sheer boredom to catch up on all my paperwork, but I've only discovered about three people in the entire world who are able to read what I've written." He flipped open his briefcase and pulled out a yellow legal-size pad. "Here," he said. "If you can read that, Ms. Fletcher, you have the job."

She took the pad from him, scarcely seeing the words scrawled in harsh, slashing lines across the pages. He didn't recognize her, she thought with a shiver of incredulity. This wasn't an act. He really had forgotten who she was. She fought an overwhelming urge to burst out laughing. This was the man who had caused her to be tried for criminal fraud. This was the man who had ruined her life, and he didn't even remember her!

"Too difficult, Ms. Fletcher?" Liam Kane sounded regretful. "I'm sorry. I have the feeling we might have worked well together, but I'm afraid I'll have to ask the personnel manager to see if he can find somebody—"

"There's no problem," she interrupted. Her heart was racing again, but the rapid pounding was no longer caused by fear. She couldn't put a name to the new emotion. Maddeningly elusive, the self-knowledge lay hidden behind some high barrier in her mind. She knew only that for the first time since Lawrence King had entered her life four years ago, she didn't feel at a disadvantage in his presence. She found it exhilarating to possess so much information about a man's past and to realize that he remembered nothing in exchange. She looked up from the report, meeting his searching gaze for the first time since her initial shock of recognition. "I don't find this draft particularly difficult to read, Mr. Kane. Would you like me to type up a rough copy for you?"

"Just read the opening couple of sentences."

"'It is widely agreed that major organizational changes

are an important part of corporate strategy. However, like many other major decisions, executive moves are too often handled outside the formal planning process.'"

He strode quickly across the room, a brief hint of admiration appearing in his eyes. "Ms. Fletcher, that was fantastic! You've just increased the total number of people able to read my handwriting by twenty-five percent! As far as I'm concerned, you're hired. I hope you'll take the job." He gave her another of his quick, engaging smiles. "I promise you that not everything I write is as pompous as the stuff you just read."

Amie looked down at the black, slashing words on the pad in front of her. His handwriting gave him away, she thought. His smiles were merely for surface consumption, and anybody who trusted those smiles was likely to get hurt badly. The truth about his character was right there on the page in front of her. Liam Kane was harsh, ruthless, decisive, relentless. But vulnerable, too, because he hadn't recognized her. She was his enemy, and he had invited her right into the heart of his camp.

She looked up from the scrawled memo. Suddenly it was desperately important for her to get this job. But she thought it would be best not to let him see how badly she wanted it. "Does a salary increase come with the promotion, Mr. Kane?" she asked evenly.

"Of course. I thought Mr. Hubert had already told you: I'm prepared to double your current salary. That's not quite as generous as it sounds, because you'll have to work three times as hard for only twice the money."

"I enjoy hard work." She was only half-listening to what he said. Her hands had finally stopped shaking, and she allowed her fingers to relax their convulsive grip on the yellow notepad he had handed her. The strange new emotion that had invaded her body was becoming stronger by the moment, although she still couldn't identify it. She decided to give up the struggle to understand why she wanted to work for Liam Kane. It was enough for the moment to know that she had been offered the job. "I'll look forward to meeting the challenge of working with you," she said, and for the first time since entering his office she smiled.

CHAPTER TWO

AMIE WAS EXHAUSTED by the time she reached her small apartment in Evanston that night. She sat at the kitchen table, toying with a bowl of soup that refused to slip down over the lump in her throat. Now that she was back in the security of her own apartment, she couldn't believe she had actually been crazy enough to accept the job of personal assistant to Liam Kane. The shock of seeing him must have upset the balance of her mind. Temporary insanity was a recognized mental condition, after all. Lots of criminals used it to excuse their behavior.

Abruptly she got up and poured the remainder of the soup into the garbage disposal. There was no point in pretending to eat. There was nobody here to be taken in by the feeble deception. What was she to do? How was she to get herself out of this mess? There was no way she could work for Liam Kane. There was no way she could tolerate the company of a man who reminded her of the past with every incisive gesture and with every subtle intonation of his mocking voice. It wasn't fair. She had worked hard over the past four years, struggling to overcome her feelings of guilt. It was a cruel joke of fate to throw Liam Kane back into her path, just when she was beginning to think she had earned the right to put the past behind her.

She went into the living room and switched on the television, staring blindly at the colorful flicker on the screen. First thing tomorrow morning she would go and see Mr. Hubert and tell him she couldn't work for Liam Kane. Perhaps she would even tell him some of the truth. She would explain how his predecessor had been an old family friend who had given her a job without asking for references. She would say . . . The tumble of her thoughts skittered to a precipitous halt. Exactly what would she say? "Excuse me, Mr. Hubert, but I can't work for Liam Kane in case he remembers that I'm a thief." She could imagine how that piece of news would go over with the kindly but conservative personnel manager.

But she wasn't a thief. It was only Liam Kane who'd accused her of fraud. She was innocent; the jury said so. Innocent but a total fool . . .

Quickly she pushed the unpleasant accusation away, her mood swinging from despair to anger as she did so. Damn Liam Kane! He had done his best to ruin her life once before. Now he seemed all set to ruin it a second time. With the clear insight provided by her anger, she realized how much she hated him. She hated his warm smiles and his calculating tawny eyes that could stare into her soul and read her mind as easily as if he had a personal window into her most secret thoughts.

She jumped up from the chair and paced the room in an effort to dissipate the tension that racked her body. She wanted revenge. It was intolerable to have to acknowledge that the man who had haunted her nightmares for all these years didn't even remember her. She wanted to humiliate Liam Kane so effectively that he would never again be able to put her out of his mind. He had inflicted four years of undeserved punishment on her, she thought bitterly, and it was time the tables were turned. She had never been guilty of the crimes of which he had accused her. She had been guilty only of being too young and too trusting and too much in love. It wasn't unreasonable of her to want to taste the pleasures of revenge. If she became his personal assistant, surely she would find some way to penetrate his seemingly impregnable defenses.

Her head had started to ache unbearably, and she pressed her forehead to the window pane. The glass felt cool against her feverish skin. She wouldn't remember the past. There was no point in remembering something that was finished. But the image of Liam Kane's harsh features thrust itself to the forefront of her mind, reminding her that today the past and the future had become inextricably interwoven.

As if the image of Liam Kane had been a key that unlocked the door to her past, a floodtide of memories rushed up and beat against the inside of her head, demanding release. The soft rain falling onto the darkened pavements blurred the outline of the streetlamps, blurring the reality of the present so that she was no longer alone in her apartment, but back in that other time when her life had been full of excitement and laughter. And Jeff.

* * *

Five years ago Amie had graduated near the top of her college class in computer science. She had always been good at math and had breezed through the computer-technology courses without much effort. That was just as well, because she'd found some of the other required courses quite tough, and she had needed to work hard in order to keep her grades up. Occasionally she wished she had more time for parties and making friends, but most often she didn't regret the long hours spent poring over her textbooks.

Her father owned the local hardware store in the small, southern Illinois farming town of Riverside. Putting her through college had been a financial struggle for her parents even though she was their only child. She was determined to repay their years of scrimping by graduating with honors. Her mother's parents hadn't been able to read or write when they arrived on the boat from Europe, and her father's parents had lost their small business during the Depression. She knew the entire family was proud of her, their first college graduate.

Amie understood how hard her parents' early lives had been, so she tried not to protest when they insisted on controlling her friendships and her way of life long after most children were allowed a measure of freedom. She lived at home in accordance with her parents' wishes and did her best not to argue when her mother asserted that boyfriends, parties, pretty clothes, and even modern music were all temptations provided by the devil.

Everything changed when she graduated and took a job in the regional office of the West Farm Insurance Company. Rebelling against her father's edicts, she moved into a tiny apartment in the center of Riverside. Life, which previously had looked somewhat gray, suddenly blazed with color and excitement. Her salary was good— especially for a woman who had previously been required to account for every penny she spent—and apartments in rural Riverside weren't expensive. For the first time in her life, she was able to splurge on stylish clothes and all the frivolities that had been denied her during the first twenty-one years of her life.

She dyed her fair hair strawberry blond and had a perm that changed the naturally silken strands into a short mop of tight, fashionably frizzy curls. She felt like a new person, not the boring Amie Fletcher who had slogged her way through four years of college. She began to experiment with makeup to go along with her new personality. She invested in a selection of glittering eyeshadows and took to keeping her nails long and polished purple.

But there was another change in her life, more important than new clothes or hairdos. Amie fell in love with her boss. Jeff Cooper was the owner of West Farm, and he was the most handsome man she had ever met. Sometimes she couldn't believe the fortunate coincidence that had brought her to his attention.

There were nine or ten young women working in the West Farm office, and Jeff had first noticed Amie when she requested an interview to point out some discrepancies in the accounts she was processing. Jeff had been very kind, teasing her gently as he explained that there were no discrepancies. She had made a mistake in her method of entry. Amie started a confused apology for her error, although she still didn't quite understand where she had gone wrong. Jeff brushed her apologies aside and invited her out to dinner. She was thrilled when he drove across the state line and took her to a nightclub in St. Louis. Their relationship progressed rapidly, though she often wondered what he saw in her. What could an inexperienced country girl offer such a handsome, sophisticated man of the world?

There was only one flaw in her happiness. Her parents didn't approve of Jeff. But Amie reminded herself that parental disapproval was nothing new. Her parents had never liked a single one of the boyfriends she had brought home for their inspection.

They met Jeff only once, at a disastrous Sunday afternoon get-together. Jeff had refused to accompany Amie's family to church. "Sermons aren't my scene," he said, giving her his most charming smile. "I'll see you at your parents' house when the service is over."

The meeting had been calamitous from start to finish. "Darling, face it," Jeff said later, dropping a careless kiss on her cheek as she apologized for the afternoon. "Your parents are straight out of another century. Basically they'd like you to sit at home obeying their every whim until *they* find the man *they* want you to marry." He pulled her along the sofa so she was thrust against his body. They were alone in his apartment, the first time Amie had agreed to come in.

"I don't think that's true," Amie protested. "I don't think my parents are at all selfish, Jeff."

"If you say so, darling. But let's not talk about them anymore. We've got far more interesting things to discuss."

"Like what?"

"Like coming with me to Chicago next weekend so we can forget about disapproving parents."

"Chicago!" she said breathlessly, filled with excitement. She had been there only once, on a short trip with some college friends, and she had been overwhelmed by the elegant sweep of the lakefront and the magnificence of the stores and public buildings. But some remnant of caution made her bite back her immediate, rapturous agreement.

"Alone?" she asked. "Just you and me? I mean, where would we stay?" She turned away from Jeff as she spoke, so that he wouldn't see she was blushing. She was angry with herself for the obvious naïveté of her questions.

Jeff laughed and held her more tightly in his arms, feathering kisses across her forehead. "Of course we would be alone," he murmured. "One of my friends has lent me his apartment in Water Tower Place. Darling, don't you want to be alone with me? You know how much I love you. You know you can trust me, Amie."

"Water Tower Place!" She couldn't disguise her awe at the prospect of staying somewhere so incredibly luxurious. She melted into Jeff's arms. This was the fourth time he had told her he loved her. She treasured the memory of each occasion. It was wonderful to think that, although her first real boyfriend was such a charming and sophisticated man, he did not hesitate to say he loved her. And how was she to keep his interest if she kept turning down all his invitations?

He kissed her passionately and hesitantly she parted her lips. She hoped he wouldn't notice that she really didn't have much experience in making love. Everything she knew, he had taught her. Jeff put his hand on her breast, caressing the curved outline with practiced skill, and she stiffened involuntarily. He had touched her breasts before, but she still wasn't quite used to his casual familiarity.

"Relax, baby," he murmured. "For God's sake don't be so uptight."

She tried to relax, although she was terribly embarrassed when his hand slid inside the front of her dress and his fingers stroked her naked flesh. She felt a strange, shivery sensation whenever he touched her so intimately, and she supposed she was feeling sexual desire. It was unfortunate that she didn't much like it. Jeff was probably right. She was stuffed full of old-fashioned inhibitions. Maybe her reactions would be more positive once she got used to the idea of making love to a man who wasn't her husband. She forced herself not to protest when his fingertips grazed her nipple.

Jeff stopped kissing her and sighed. "You sure are full of hang-ups, baby," he said. "Forget about your parents, Amie, and all the out-of-date morality they shoved into you. Life is meant to be enjoyed, not worried about."

"I know," she said, deliberately pressing herself back against his body. After all, she reasoned silently, there was nothing wrong with making love to a man who loved you, just as there was nothing wrong with going away with somebody you loved. She was twenty-one; she had been a legal adult for three years. She was certainly old enough to decide whether or not she wanted to remain a virgin. As Jeff had pointed out, this was the end of the twentieth century, not the middle of the nineteenth. Virginity was no longer a requirement for marriage.

They drove to Chicago on Saturday morning. The apartment in Water Tower Place was the last word in luxury. Amie was thrilled that she had dredged up the courage to accept Jeff's invitation. The day passed in a blaze of excitement. Together they whirled through the department stores, and then Jeff took her to a fabulous

Italian restaurant for dinner. Afterward they went to a nightclub that was so elegant and expensive that Amie was almost afraid to step out onto the dance floor. She understood—really understood—for the first time just how provincial Riverside's social life must seem to a man like Jeff. He had traveled to so many interesting places and met so many fascinating people that it made his love for her all the more remarkable.

Her legs were wobbly and her feet seemed to be floating an inch or so above the pavement by the time they returned to the apartment in Water Tower Place. Amie's stomach was churning with some very strange sensations, and she found herself giggling a lot.

"I think I've had too much to drink," she confided to Jeff. "What was that brown stuff we were drinking? I hope it wasn't whiskey or anything; I've never drunken whiskey."

"It was sherry. Imported sherry."

She giggled again. Jeff's arm was tight around her body, and when his fingers rested possessively against her breast, she didn't mind. She nestled her head on his shoulder as the elevator carried them up to the fortieth floor. "We're like eagles," she said as he opened the apartment door. "Tonight we're going to sleep in the sky."

"Sure. Don't worry about a thing, baby. Leave everything to me." He walked straight through the living room, leading her into the bedroom. The spread had already been taken off the king-size bed, and the sheets were turned back invitingly. She kicked off her shoes and collapsed against the pillows.

"I'm tired," she said.

Jeff's eyes narrowed slightly. "Let me help you get

undressed," he said smoothly. "That's a new dress, isn't it? You don't want to ruin it."

He pulled her off the bed and began, very gently, to slide open the zipper. He kissed the back of her neck, thrusting the dress off her shoulders with practiced skill. The sudden chill of cold air against her midriff dissipated the effects of the alcohol for a moment, and Amie felt a rush of fear.

"Jeff," she whispered. "Jeff, I'm not ready for this. I'm scared."

She felt his impatience, although his smile didn't waver. "Come on, darling, this isn't the time to get cold feet. Let me show you what lovemaking's all about. Isn't it time you grew up and became a woman?"

"Do you love me, Jeff?"

"Baby, of course I do. I adore you." He finished removing her bra and quickly unfastened his shirt, pulling off his tie with swift, efficient movements. He took Amie into his arms and pushed her back toward the bed. When her legs were pressed right up against the bedframe, he began to kiss her. Before she knew it, she was lying on the peach-colored sheets with Jeff's body stretched on top of her.

She felt another moment of panic when she realized that, even now, she still wasn't experiencing any of the magical sensations she had read about. She saw no stars when Jeff kissed her. She heard no music when he stroked her skin. She lay, stiff and nervous, as he tried to coax her into some semblance of passion. She did her best to pretend that she was responding, although passion was hard to fake when you had never experienced it. She bit her lip until it bled to prevent herself from crying out with pain at the moment Jeff finally possessed her. She told herself the pain was worth it. An accomplished lover like Jeff deserved an equally skillful partner. It wasn't his fault that she had failed so dismally to respond to his expert caresses.

She awoke the following morning with a faint feeling of nausea and a splitting headache. But she told herself she had no regrets. This trip was worth it because Jeff smiled at her now with new intimacy, murmuring words of love as they made the drive back from the city through the flat, empty farmlands of southern Illinois.

"There's a new guy starting at the office on Monday," Jeff mentioned casually as he dropped Amie outside her apartment in Riverside. "Lawrence King. I hired him on the recommendation of one of my friends. He's supposed to be a crackerjack insurance salesman. Be nice to him, Amie. We could use a salesman with a bit of life in him. New sales have been badly off recently."

"That's because you're spending so much time working in the home office. Everybody says you're the best salesman for miles around."

He lifted his shoulders in a modest shrug. "I wish I could be out in the field, but somebody has to catch up on all the administrative work and all the legal mumbo jumbo the government insists on. Just because we're selling medical insurance, the stooges in Washington seem to think I have nothing to do but fill out forms and answer questionnaires in triplicate! And somebody has to see that the money we collect is wisely invested, since people are relying on us to pay their medical bills." He gave another one of his endearingly modest smiles. "I'm in charge of West Farm Insurance, so I guess the investment decisions have to be mine. We don't want the fund to go broke."

"As if it could. The figures you gave me last month looked terrific . . . although there was one thing I wanted to ask you about the premium payments. The way we're entering them into the computer, you can't tell which fund they're assigned to, Jeff."

He leaned over and kissed her. "Don't worry about things you don't understand, darling. That's the way the government wants us to keep the books, so we just have to do what they say. See you tomorrow, beautiful." She got out of the car. "Amie!" he called softly as she walked to the entrance of her apartment.

"Yes?"

"How about a trip to Jamaica next weekend? There's an insurance convention I ought to attend."

She was weak-kneed with excitement. "Jeff! Jamaica! I can't believe it."

"Believe it, honey. Go plan what you'll pack for a weekend of tropical sunshine, and stop worrying about the numbers you put into the computer. Worrying's my job." He gave her another smile and a quick wave before roaring off down the street, the car's engine loud in the silence of Riverside on a Sunday night.

From the first moment she saw him, Amie disliked Lawrence King. She found his physical presence disturbing in a way that she couldn't account for. He wasn't handsome like Jeff, but she sensed a latent power hidden behind his austere features. His hair was very dark and thick, but his eyes weren't brown as she would have expected them to be. They were a curious tawny shade that in some lights seemed to take on an almost golden gleam. When his gaze rested on her, she felt naked. Not in her body, but in her mind, as if Lawrence could strip away all her petty pretenses and see right through to her soul.

She was very glad that Lawrence was a salesman and often out in the field making calls. She felt uneasy whenever he came into the office. She tried to put him right out of her mind, but she seemed to have some sort of personal radar system that warned her whenever he was near. She always knew he was in the room long before she actually saw him. When he was out of the office, she found him hard to forget. Even when she was lying with Jeff on the beach in Jamaica, Lawrence's image thrust itself to the forefront of her mind. He seemed to be looking at her accusingly, his firm mouth turned downward in faint distaste. She didn't enjoy her trip nearly as much as she should have.

Unfortunately, as far as Amie was concerned, Lawrence seemed to be fascinated by computers. He was a frustrated computer buff, he told her with one of the smiles she disliked so much. If he was in the office, he never failed to pay her a visit. He would watch her inputting new figures into the system, asking her question after question about the techniques and procedures of keeping accounts in the computer age. His questions made her uneasy. When she tried to explain to him what she was doing, she sometimes had to stumble to a halt because all too often she knew that the procedure she was following didn't conform to any system she had been taught in college. I must talk to Jeff, she would tell herself. It was all very well for the government to issue instructions that West Farm was supposed to obey, but Jeff couldn't realize how inadequate their systems were. She tried to broach the subject with him a couple of times, but somehow he always dismissed her questions without resolving her problems satisfactorily.

She temporarily gave up worrying about the inadequacies of the program she was using and began to feed the month's sales figures into the system. She heard the door open and knew Lawrence had come into the office. She stiffened as she felt his watchful presence at her shoulder.

"What are you up to this morning?" he asked cheerfully.

"Nothing. I mean I'm working, of course." She hated the way he always contrived to make her sound foolish. He was invariably polite, but in some indefinable way he made her nervous.

"Computers are fascinating tools for accountants," he said, watching her fingers fly over the keyboard. "They're not like old-fashioned account books where you had a permanent record of all the steps in any financial transaction. A computer only prints out what its told—usually nothing more than the end result. The systems the accountant has used to produce the final figures often leave no trace. Most of the entries an accountant makes today are no more than flashes of light, brief electronic impulses that have no independent life and leave no record behind."

"I've been aware of that since my first year of college."

"Yes, I'm sure you have. And I expect your professors pointed out to you how important it is to build safeguards into every system so that you can trace possible errors back to their source."

"Yes. We had that hammered into us every other semester. Actually, I'm a bit busy today, Lawrence."

He refused to take the hint, perching casually on the

corner of her desk. She kept her gaze fixed firmly on the display screen. She could feel her cheeks burn with two spots of color where his eyes seemed to be boring into her.

"You do all the accounts here, don't you, Amie?"

"Not really. I'm just responsible for the company's balance sheet. Sharon makes all the checks out for individual claims and all that sort of thing." Inexplicably defensive, she added, "Jeff set up the company's accounting system according to government regulations, Lawrence. My job title may be chief accountant, but really I'm nothing but a glorified clerk. It's my first job, after all."

"Don't put yourself down, my dear. You're highly trained, a college graduate."

She was silent.

"Of course," he continued, just as if she had spoken, "computers have opened up a marvelous new era for crooks. Have you read about any of the spectacular computer frauds that have been perpetrated during the past decade? There was the one in Los Angeles where a bank clerk successfully absconded with a million dollars. Nobody realized he'd fixed the books, but he gave himself away by spending too much money too fast. His friends began to wonder how he could afford two fancy sports cars and trips to Europe every couple of months. How was your trip to Jamaica, by the way?"

"It was very enjoyable," she said tersely. "What do *you* do with yourself on weekends, Lawrence?" she asked, anxious to change the subject. "I understand you're married, but I haven't seen your wife around town."

He got off the desk. "No," he said curtly. "My wife's sick." There was silence for a moment or two before he spoke again. "She has bone cancer."

Amie's fingers stopped their nervous key-tapping. She looked directly at Lawrence and saw the hint of pain hidden behind his stern expression. "I'm so very sorry," she said softly. "Is there any way I can help? Run errands, or just visit with your wife? It must be lonely for her, being a newcomer to the town."

His gaze caught hers, and for the first time she saw how warm and caring his eyes could be. "Thank you," he said. "But my wife's in the hospital and her family is staying nearby. She isn't quite up to receiving other visitors."

"I'm truly sorry, Lawrence. I hope...I hope she's not in great pain?" Amie was unexpectedly devastated by the grim implication of his words.

"My wife is a very brave woman," he said. There was silence in the room for a moment; then Lawrence moved away from her desk. "I won't keep you from your accounts any longer," he said. "I'm sure those figures are important."

He strode across the small room, banging the door as he went out. It was the first time Amie could recall him expressing any hint of emotion. Normally he seemed to keep his feelings under almost unnatural control. Amie turned back to the keyboard with a grimace. Lawrence was an uncomfortable man to be around, and she certainly didn't want to start feeling sympathy for him, even if his wife was dying. Somehow she knew that it would be very dangerous to allow herself to start liking Lawrence King.

Jeff invited her to a party in Springfield that weekend, and Amie accepted eagerly. Recently she had become aware of considerable strain in her relationship with him. Lawrence's searching questions had focused all her own doubts about the accounting system, and she was angry that Jeff refused to take her objections seriously. She had already reminded him that she was fully trained even if she was inexperienced. "You're *paying* me to point out deficiencies and catch errors before they snowball into something serious," she said to him, her voice tight with frustration.

"Cool it, baby," he replied with infuriating condescension. "Try not to be a nag."

They came close to having a full-scale argument during the short drive to Springfield. Perhaps because of this, Amie found the party less than enjoyable. Most of Jeff's friends seemed to drink a great deal, and she didn't think that getting drunk was the best way to have a good time. She could barely tolerate Jeff's lovemaking that night when the party was over. Her emotions were so churned up that her body seemed frozen into virtual numbness. She didn't bother to pretend satisfaction as she usually did, but he gave no indication that he noticed any difference in her responses. So much for her powers of faking passion, she thought wryly and turned her face into the pillow. Jeff was already asleep, so he didn't notice when she got up from the bed and crossed to the window. She sat staring out into the deserted motel parking lot far into the night.

Jeff left her outside her apartment on Sunday night. She was glad he didn't press for an invitation to come inside. She felt a desperate need to be alone to think.

Unfortunately, she discovered that her thinking had occurred too late. When she went into the office on Monday morning, she found the small building crawling with law-enforcement officers. "What's happened?" she asked the receptionist, feeling sick with fright. At some deeply hidden level of her subconscious she was afraid she knew exactly what the problem was.

"They won't give us any details." Mrs. Simon's plump face was white with strain. Good jobs were hard to come by in Riverside. "Something about a fraud. I heard them saying there's no money in one of the funds. People have been sending in medical bills and they haven't been paid."

The sickness in Amie's stomach swelled. Forcing the nausea away, she hurried past the receptionist and went into her own office. She found the computer guarded by a fresh-faced young man who looked embarrassed by his task.

"I'm afraid you can't touch anything in here, miss," he said, gesturing to her desk. "All this stuff—the disks and the software and so on—has been impounded as evidence."

"Evidence?"

He shifted uncomfortably. "The state government received a lot of complaints, miss. Hospitals were reporting that their claims for reimbursement hadn't been met. And there were individual complaints too. Some people who thought they were insured have found themselves stuck with huge bills for operations and such. There's no money left in the funds handled by West Farm."

"There must be some mistake! There has to be an explanation for the delays. Perhaps we haven't been processing payment checks fast enough. I checked the figures on the operating fund last month. We have at least half a million dollars in negotiable assets!"

"Are you sure?" Lawrence King walked into the room. "Are you prepared to back that statement with concrete evidence, Ms. Fletcher?" She whirled around at the sound of his voice, feeling the edge of the desk pushing into the small of her back. His gaze seemed to pin her to the desk like a trapped butterfly.

His eyes were fixed on her mouth. She opened her parched lips, not sure she would be able to speak. "What's all this got to do with you? You're a salesman. You only just joined the company."

Silently he reached into his pocket and pulled out a plastic-covered identification card.

"You're not a salesman; you're a federal agent," she said flatly. Her voice hovered somewhere between a whisper and a croak. "But there's no name on your card, only a picture."

"For obvious reasons I don't use my real name when I'm on a case. I'm allowed to testify in court without revealing my true identity."

"You've been investigating West Farm! All those questions you asked me . . ." Her voice trailed away into silence.

"I'm retained by the federal government to investigate high-level computer fraud, although this case didn't really need an agent with a great deal of training. Mr. Cooper didn't bother to rig the programs in any very sophisticated way."

"Mr. Cooper? Jeff isn't responsible for defrauding the company; he can't be!" She made her denial all the more vehement because she wasn't at all sure it was true.

He looked at her coldly. "In our judgment, Mr. Cooper has been operating the funds as a source of personal income for at least the last two years. He's already under arrest."

"I don't believe it!" she said fiercely. "He couldn't

have manipulated the funds; he wouldn't do such a thing! I mean, people depend on West Farm to pay their medical bills. Poor Jeff! Why have you picked on him as your scapegoat?"

She couldn't interpret the strange expression that flickered across Lawrence's harsh features. Abruptly he turned to leave. "If I were you," he said, "I'd save my sympathy. I think you're going to need it."

A day later he came to her apartment with two local policemen. They had both known her since she was a child, and neither of them would meet her eyes. In contrast, Lawrence looked straight at her, his tawny gaze devoid of emotion. His voice was clear, crisp, and chillingly remote as he told her she was under arrest for complicity in a fraudulent insurance scheme. In the same chilling monotone he informed her of her right to remain silent and her right to a lawyer's representation.

He spoke to her only once again. He came up to her when she was at the local police station, trying to clean her hands of the ink the policeman had used to take her fingerprints.

"Do you want me to call your parents?" he asked.

She couldn't look at him. "No, thank you."

He walked away without saying another word.

She didn't see "Lawrence King" again until the start of her trial. He appeared as a witness for the prosecution, recounting with devastating precision the many conversations he had had with Amie about West Farm's computer programs. By the time he finished his testimony, she could virtually hear the cell door clanging shut behind her. But she had reached the point where even jail seemed almost preferable to any more time spent in the crowded local courtroom. She had learned to dread the covert inspection by a hundred pairs of curious eyes. She felt unbearable guilt every time she saw the hunched, defeated figures of her parents seated across the aisle.

She was too numb to feel more than a twinge of surprise when under cross-examination her defense counsel persuaded King to admit that perhaps Amie had been foolish rather than criminal. Under the circumstances, Amie supposed she should be grateful that the jury was prepared to consider her a fool. They returned a verdict of Not Guilty after less than an hour of deliberation.

The trial was over. Legally she was a free woman. Lawrence King left the courtroom without so much as a glance in her direction. But she had been looking at him when the jury delivered its verdict, and she knew she would never forget the flash of deep emotion that darkened his features when the foreman pronounced her innocent. Whatever the law declared, Lawrence King undoubtedly considered her guilty.

CHAPTER THREE

THE TRIAL HAD been a long time ago, Amie thought, brushing a hand over her eyes as the rain-washed streets of Evanston came back into focus. She was no longer the heedless girl who had imagined herself in love with Jeff Cooper. She had grown up with a vengeance over the past four years.

Her parents had urged her to leave Riverside as soon as the trial was over, and she had complied with their wishes. She had been in no state to make decisions for herself, so she didn't protest when her father approached an old friend who was personnel manager at the National Development Corporation in Chicago. She was offered a position as a junior clerk and she accepted at once, thanking her father politely for his efforts on her behalf.

She understood why her parents didn't want her to

stay in Riverside. They were stalwarts of the local community and devout members of their church. She was
their only child and they wanted to love her, but she had
betrayed their values and shattered their proud dreams.

She left home a week after the trial ended. She stepped
onto the bus with her head held high, but inside her heart
was bleeding. In the four years since she had moved to
the city, she'd never once returned to Riverside. During
her first lonely months she had hoped against hope that
her parents would invite her for a visit, but the letter she
longed for never came. Her parents wrote her polite notes
at Christmas and on her birthday, but they never said
they missed her or suggested coming to Chicago.

She caught sight of her reflection in the dark pane of
the window and sighed, not quite knowing why. She had
lost so much weight during the last four years that she
now looked frail rather than fashionably slender, and her
severe hairstyle emphasized her high cheekbones and the
faint hollows beneath them. It was difficult to believe
her hair had once been a wild mop of frizzy curls and
that she had scoured the Riverside stores searching for
the latest and most outrageous fashions. If only her parents could see her now, she thought wistfully. Maybe
they'd finally approve of the way she looked and the
way she was living.

Her current lifestyle bore no relationship to those re-
bellious months she had spent with Jeff. She didn't date,
because she no longer trusted her judgment in men. And
women usually misinterpreted her wariness and imagined
her to be aloof and cold. She often thought that the most
interesting part of her week was the time she spent on
Saturday mornings working at a special center for the
handicapped. She used her knowledge of computers to

help train blind teenagers in the operation of sophisticated electronic telephone equipment. The director of the center and his wife were the only real friends she had made in Chicago, and even to them she hadn't dared confide the truth about her past.

She turned abruptly from the window and walked with sudden briskness into her tiny bedroom. The time had come to make a decisive change in her life. This morning fate had decreed that her past and her future should come together, and she intended to pick up the challenge thrown at her feet. Liam Kane had invited her back into his life, and she would use the opportunity to plan his downfall. After four years of loneliness, revenge would taste very sweet.

The next morning, Amie walked with unusual jauntiness into the spacious lobby of the National Development Corporation building.

The personnel manager and his young assistant happened to be arriving at the same time. "Morning, Amie," Mr. Hubert said. "I was delighted to hear from the president that he'd offered you the job."

Amie smiled. "I'm looking forward to starting work for Mr. Kane," she said. The knowledge of her secret plan was like an intoxicant bubbling through her veins, and she couldn't stop from giving them both another radiant smile. "Thank you again for recommending me."

"My pleasure." She wasn't quite out of earshot when the personnel manager said to his assistant, "Do you know, I don't think I've ever seen Amie Fletcher smile before? I never realized until just now what an attractive woman she could be if she'd only shed a few inhibitions."

His assistant laughed. "Are you saying there's really

a passionate heart beating beneath those starched white blouses? Come on, boss, it's too early in the morning for bad jokes."

Amie paid little attention to their banter because her thoughts were fixed on her forthcoming encounter with Liam Kane. Her spirits continued to soar as swiftly as the high-speed elevator carrying her to the twentieth floor. Catching herself humming a tune under her breath as she hurried along the corridor to her new office, she stopped, feeling annoyance as soon as she realized what she was doing. She paused outside the door of the outer office to draw a quick, calming gulp of air.

There was no sign of Liam Kane. It wasn't yet eight o'clock, and she was counting on having a good half hour to herself before he arrived. She hung her light-weight spring jacket in an empty closet, then checked the supplies in her desk with swift efficiency. There was a mountain of unopened mail stacked in a tray on her desk, but she wasn't sure she should open it. She didn't want to overstep the limits of her position on her very first day. She tested the file cabinets, which were all locked, and decided to familiarize herself with the duplicating equipment that was standing in a corner of her office.

She had no warning of his arrival. After four years she had forgotten how silently he could move. "Good morning, Ms. Fletcher," he said from somewhere behind her back.

She managed to compose her face in the split second before she turned to face him. "Good morning, Mr. Kane."

"I'm glad you're here early," he said. "It's a promising start." The smile he gave her would have melted almost any female heart. But not hers. "Come into my office and let's run through my schedule for the next week. That's as good a way as any to get acquainted."

She picked up her notepad and a leather-bound book that had the word *Appointments* stamped in flowing gold leaf across the front cover. When they were inside his office, she stood perfectly still, her face expressionless as she waited for his instructions. Inside, her stomach churned with excitement. She hadn't felt so vibrantly alive in years.

"Please sit down," he said. "This is likely to be a long session because I want to fill you in on my plans for the next couple of weeks." His eyes caught hers before she could turn away. "You're looking somewhat tense, Ms. Fletcher. Not regretting your decision to come and work for the corporate ogre, are you?"

"I believe I have a naturally pale complexion, Mr. Kane. I'm not at all regretting my decision to come and work for you. In fact, I'm looking forward to it. I think working as your secretary will allow me to use the full range of my talents."

She had to drop her gaze and smother the start of a smile when she finished speaking. Oh, but it was wonderful to know that every word she said had a double meaning, while Mr. Kane—*Mr. Know-it-all, Investigator Kane*—could only understand the superficial significance of her words. She felt a surge of triumph, but she was wise enough not to look up until she was sure she had banished all trace of it from her expression.

The tawny eyes surveyed her for no more than a second. She told herself she must have imagined the faint spark of something—interest? anger? wariness?—that she had detected briefly in his gaze.

He leaned back in his chair, apparently completely

relaxed, no hint of anything but friendliness in his eyes. "Tell me, Ms. Fletcher, as a comparative old-timer to a real newcomer, how do you like living in Chicago? I saw from your personnel file that you moved here only four years ago."

She wasn't prepared for the personal question, and for a moment she completely lost her poise. "I . . . er . . . I . . ." She cleared her throat and tried again. "It's an interesting city," she said. "Although the winters seem to go on rather a long time."

The seductive laughter she had noticed the day before returned to deepen his voice. "I was warned before I took this job that I'd better learn to enjoy winter sports! Do you ski, Ms. Fletcher?"

"I've done some cross-country skiing," she replied, turning away from the warmth of his smile. Liam Kane was a man who had previously made his living by pretending to be somebody that he was not. She would be a fool to allow herself to believe that his smiles were genuine. She needed to remember every minute of every day that Liam Kane was her enemy. She opened the leather-bound appointment book. "You certainly seem to have a busy program over the next few weeks, Mr. Kane."

He accepted her change of conversation without comment. "I'm afraid so. And I'm relying on you to keep me strictly on schedule. Most of these meetings shouldn't last longer than fifteen minutes, and I'll need you to interrupt each session with discreet reminders about my next meeting. Can I count on you to play dragon to my ogre?"

"I'll do my best, Mr. Kane."

There was a wry twist to his smile as he glanced at her. "I'm sure your best will be highly successful, Ms.

Fletcher. Now, about tomorrow's meeting with the president of our Mexican subsidiary. He's here to discuss license renewals. Could you find the files on the original agreement and bring them to me? You may have a little difficulty. Your predecessor didn't like filing, and as far as I can see, she did as little as possible. That was only one of the reasons I didn't want to take her on as my secretary. Fortunately, she was close to retirement anyway."

"Fortunate for me, at any rate," Amie said neutrally. "Would you like me to find the Mexican agreements right away?"

"Please."

It took her twenty minutes to unearth the papers he wanted. She was just pulling them from the back of a drawer when he walked into her office. "Any luck with that Mexican file?" he asked.

"I have it here, Mr. Kane."

He stood beside her, spreading the contents of the folder over the top of the filing cabinet. She started to move away. "Don't go," he said. "I want to be sure everything I need is here."

She stood rigidly at his side, aware of a peculiar suffocating sensation that constricted her throat and made her body tremble. He reached for one of the scrawled sheets of figures and his hand brushed down the length of her arm. For a moment she thought she was going to scream. She had never realized before that hate could cause such an intense physical reaction.

"Everything's here," he said. "Are you ready to go over my schedule, Ms. Fletcher?"

"Yes, yes, of course." With the rigid powers of concentration she had developed over the last few years, she forced her mind to shut out everything except the work at hand. There would be time to relax later. Later...when she had exacted her revenge.

Sometimes during the next few weeks she wondered if her plans for vengeance would ever move beyond the first stage of getting Liam Kane to trust her. She quickly discovered that working for him was a very different proposition from working for the elderly sales manager who had been her previous boss. Liam was cool and low keyed in his approach to his work, but at the same time he was ruthlessly hard-driving of himself and the people around him. His understanding of business problems was so quick and incisive that Amie began to feel she was always two steps behind in her own work and at least a dozen steps behind him.

She stretched her skills to their outer limits in order to cope with Liam's demands, and gradually she found herself taking pride in anticipating his needs. She waged a personal battle with the mountains of paperwork generated by his meetings, and little by little she found she was winning.

Quite often when she stumbled back to her apartment late at night she would realize that another whole day had gone by in which she had not once given a thought to her plans for punishing him. She tried to comfort herself with the promise that she would turn her attention to revenge as soon as she had her work under control. She tried never to think about the subtle pleasure she was deriving from learning to do a difficult job. She cut her thoughts short when she began to wonder why she found the long hours working alone with Liam so exhilarating.

On Monday morning, the start of her fifth week as

Liam's secretary, Amie arrived at the office extra early, although her head was aching fiercely after a totally sleepless night. Today, she swore to herself, she was going to organize her desk before Liam arrived. For once, she was going to live up to her reputation as the cool, efficient Ms. Fletcher who always had everything under control. In the past couple of weeks her facade had suffered some nearly fatal cracks. It was time to get her mask firmly back in place again. It was definitely time to remember why she had taken this job.

She sorted through the mail which had arrived on Saturday and cleared away a mound of papers that had accumulated during the hectic Friday afternoon rush. She placed a quick call to the travel agent confirming Liam's evening flight to Florida. He would be out of the office all day Tuesday, talking to county officials in Florida. He was deeply involved in negotiations for land on which to build a middle-income housing project in western Florida. It was a project he had suggested to the board of directors when he became president, and the realization of a big loss or a comfortable profit depended very much on the terms he managed to negotiate. Amie began to group together the documents relating to the project, including some preliminary drawings that had just been delivered by the senior draftsman.

At the sound of swift footsteps in the carpeted hallway, she felt a strange curl of emotion in the pit of her stomach. She forced herself to continue checking through the piles of paper on her desk. She ignored the fact that her pulse had started to race with a tingling eagerness, and got up to file the few documents remaining on her desk.

She sensed the exact moment of his arrival in her

office without any need to turn around, but she feigned unawareness and bent down to put a file into the bottom drawer.

"Good morning, Amie. It's good to see you're hard at it already."

It was the first time he had called her anything other than "Ms. Fletcher," and she discovered that she liked the sound of her name spoken in his deep, clear voice. The discovery bothered her and she stood up, straightening quickly from her crouching position by the low file drawer. A sudden wave of dizziness overcame her, and she had to cling momentarily to the support of a nearby chair.

He was at her side almost immediately, his arm around her waist, his hand smoothing a stray wisp of hair from her eyes. "Hey, Amie," he said gently. "What's all this about? You've turned the same shade of gray as the file cabinet."

She couldn't help swaying against him, but she told herself it was only because she was still dizzy. His arms came around her protectively. "Lean on me while we go into my office," he said. "You've obviously been overdoing it. Come and rest on the sofa."

"I'll be all right," she said, recovering her voice, although she still felt surprisingly weak. It was comfortable resting against the rough surface of his jacket, but she forced herself to pull away. She didn't want to find Liam Kane comforting. "I just have a bit of a headache," she said. "I'll take a couple of aspirins."

Paying no attention to her protests, he ushered her into his office, one hand supporting her elbow and the other arm firmly around her waist. He made her lie down on the sofa, arranging a cushion behind her head. "You don't look gray anymore," he said. "Now you look white. For heaven's sake, Amie, why did you come in today? You aren't well."

"I couldn't stay home," she said faintly. "You have so much to do before you leave tonight for Florida."

"Nothing that's worth fainting over," he answered dryly. He walked to the phone and pressed an intercom switch. "Send up some tea, please, as quickly as you can."

He put down the phone and returned to sit on the sofa. She could feel the muscles of his thigh pressing against the length of her leg, and she wondered if he was aware that her body trembled in immediate reaction to his touch. "Why didn't you tell me I've been working you too hard?" he said. "You look exhausted, Amie, and it's only the beginning of the week."

Everything would be all right, she thought, if he would just move away. She couldn't bear it when he was so near. The pressure of his body against her legs made her feel feverish, light-headed, as if she might do something crazy at any moment, something insane, like throwing herself into his arms and asking him to hold her. "Would you please move?" she said, doing her best to sound totally in command of herself. "I stood up too fast, Mr. Kane, that's all. I'm okay now."

He looked directly into her eyes and smiled. Even though she had seen that smile work its magic on at least a hundred employees, she had to turn away to resist its charm. "Still determined to play Wonder Woman?" he said. "At least stay put until you've had something to drink."

As he spoke, a knock at the door announced the arrival of their tea. Liam took the tray from the elderly woman and set it down on his desk. He filled two cups and carried them over to the sofa, then sat down beside Amie and talked quietly about his weekend fishing trip while she drank.

Her cup rattled when she finally replaced it in the saucer, and she willed her hands back to steadiness. "I'm ready to start work now, Mr. Kane."

"My name's Liam," he said. "I'd like you to use it. If you're up to working again, come over to the conference table. I need your help on the West Florida project."

"Yes, of course." She returned her cup to the tray. When she sat down at the conference table, she took care not to place her chair too close to his. Her reactions to Liam Kane today seemed inexplicable, and she felt even more tense when he spread the papers over the table and his hand accidentally brushed hers. Silently she moved her hands to her lap.

Liam looked at her quizzically. "Are you sure you can read these figures from that far away, Amie?"

"Yes, thank you."

"As you can see, these are cost analyses for the West Florida project. It would be a big help if you could run my calculations through the computer and come up with the critical variables in construction costs. I've done all the technical analyses, so it's simply a matter of feeding figures into my personal desk computer and waiting for it to give you some answers. Do you think you can handle that?"

"I'm not very familiar with the new personal computer systems used by this company," she said, hoping her voice wasn't betraying too much of what she was feeling.

Computers were a dangerous subject to be discussing with Liam Kane, and her throat began to tighten.

"Why aren't you familiar with our computer systems?"

"Nobody in the sales department ever asked me to run a program," she said stiffly. "There are lots of people in the project analysis department who could make the estimates for you."

"But I understood from the personnel manager that you were trained to work with computers before you joined our company. That was one of the reasons I hired you in the first place, you know. You can be invaluable to me once you learn to make fast, accurate cost estimates. Besides, these figures are highly confidential, and I know I can trust you to treat them with absolute discretion. I don't want my projections tossed around headquarters by some junior computer programmer."

She felt a deep flush of color darken the pallor of her cheeks. Liam was saying he trusted her! After one short month, the first part of her plan was already successful—Liam was prepared to give her important and confidential information!

"I suppose I could try to work on the calculations tomorrow, when you're out of town," she said, not meeting his eyes. If only he would stop staring at her! She felt sure her cheeks were still stained with a flush of excitement. Just you wait, Mr. Investigator Kane, she thought. If you only knew it, in giving me these confidential papers, you're handing over the perfect means of revenge. Amie felt certain that she possessed sufficient technical knowledge to fudge the calculations so that his final estimates would turn out hopelessly wide of the mark. She was aware of a tremendous sense of relief in realizing that her revenge could be so easily accom-

plished. Working for Liam Kane hadn't turned out at all
as she'd expected, and she wanted to get away from him
as soon as possible.

Amie stretched out her hand, relieved to see that it
was quite steady now despite the jangle of her emotions.
"If you'll give me the papers," she said, "I'll do my best
to come up with some answers for you."

"Thank you." He watched her walk across the room,
his body tense, and called her back just as she reached
the door. "Amie, I don't think I've taken the time to tell
you how much I appreciate the tremendous job you've
done for me so far. I know I wouldn't have accomplished
half as much this past month without you to take care of
all the administrative details. I'm grateful, more grateful
than I can say. You're easily the most competent secretary I've ever had."

She felt her body suffuse with pleasure until she realized the inappropriateness of that reaction. She didn't
want Liam Kane's praise—she hated him. She mustn't
forget that she was holding the means of revenge literally
in her hands. "I'm glad you're pleased with my work,"
she said. "I hope to be even more successful in the future." She turned away abruptly. Today, for some reason,
she could derive little pleasure from her subtle double-
entendres.

She worked on the West Florida estimate all Tuesday
while Liam was out of town. Before she started, she
knew the task would be a long one. She began to feed
numbers into the computer as soon as she arrived at the
office, working the projections through as accurately as
she possibly could. That way, she told herself, she would
be able to see where crucial changes in the estimates

could be made. A few well-buried "mistakes," she thought gleefully, and the West Florida project would turn out to be a major loss for the company instead of a substantial profit.

It was four years since she had worked with any sort of computer, but although there had been vast strides forward in technology, Liam's personal desk model was relatively simple to understand for somebody with her advanced training. At first she refused to admit how much pleasure she got from seeing the detailed structure of the estimate flowering into a pattern under her touch. Gradually, as the hours passed, she began to admit how impressed she was with the elegant simplicity of Liam's work. As she built more complex projections onto his base figures, she finally realized how much she had missed her profession. There was something very gratifying about reducing complex, seemingly unrelated facts to manageable blocks of information.

It was late in the evening before she finished the entire series of estimates. She stared for several minutes at the columns of bright green figures on the screen in front of her and knew that there was no way in the world she could falsify those calculations. With a twinge of horror, she realized that although she hadn't been guilty of a crime four years ago, she had nearly been guilty of one today. She forced herself to face up to the fact that she had actually been contemplating defrauding the National Development Corporation in order to satisfy her personal wish for revenge against Liam Kane.

Her hands shook on the computer keys as she made the series of commands that ordered the computer to print out her calculations. With sudden unwelcome clarity she saw the unavoidable flaw in all of her previous plans for revenge. If she used her position of trust to betray Liam, she would inevitably harm the National Development Corporation. Liam was president of the company, and any mistake that was big enough to cause his downfall was bound to be big enough to hurt the company.

Amie's hands were cold but steady as she removed the printed sheets from the computer and organized them into a neat stack. Thank God, she had come to her senses before her personal feud with Liam Kane totally corrupted her ethics. How could she have planned to penalize the employees and stockholders of National Development? How could she have been so blind that she didn't see where her schemes were leading her?

She left the stack of printout sheets on Liam's desk. It was past seven o'clock, and she felt cocooned in the muffled silence of the nearly-deserted building. She stretched wearily, then walked over to the window and looked out at the lights gradually brightening the city buildings. She took off her glasses and rubbed her eyes. A thick strand of hair had worked its way loose from her tightly-coiled braids and she pushed it back with careless fingers. Fatigue made her clumsy. A few pins fell out, allowing two thick wings of hair to escape confinement and curve loosely around her shoulders. With an impatient exclamation, she pulled out the remaining pins and massaged the back of her neck, then shook her head in an attempt to relieve the tension of too many hours spent hunched over a computer keyboard.

She couldn't guess how long Liam had been standing there looking at her before she became aware of his presence. She felt a sudden compelling urge to turn from the window, and there he was. They stared at one another in silence, and she wondered if she imagined the brief flash of emotion that darkened his eyes. She hurriedly pushed her hair away from her face and swallowed hard, trying to moisten vocal chords that were inexplicably dry. "Liam . . ." she said. "I didn't expect to see you here tonight."

Her efforts to speak normally weren't very successful. Her voice produced nothing like its usual cool tones. Realizing that she wasn't wearing her glasses, she shoved them back on, feeling calmer as soon as her eyes were concealed behind the tinted lenses. "H–how are you, Liam?" she asked. "I mean, how were your meetings?"

"Better than we expected. We made good progress in our discussions about tax concessions. A couple of the local officials are obviously being paid off by somebody to obstruct our plans, but I'd guess most of the people we're dealing with are honest, and that's a promising beginning."

"Yes, I'm sure it must be. How were . . . that is, did you have to field any especially tough questions?"

"Well, we encountered an irate delegation from the local environmental protection group, who told me they were fighting to save the county's swamp lands. As far as I can make out, in practical terms that means they're encouraging the breeding of mosquitoes. And when the environmentalists finished, I had to face the usual barrage of questions about storm drains and sewage pipes. I sometimes think I spend half my waking life talking about septic fields and sludge disposal."

Amie laughed before she could stop herself. "Houses do need drains, after all. And I guess the swamps do breed alligators as well as mosquitoes."

His gaze rested for a moment on the soft curve of her mouth. "They certainly do," he said. "Is that supposed to be a point in favor of the environmentalists?" He loosened his tie and undid the top button of his shirt. "God, but I'm tired. I'm hungry, too. If there's no rampaging boyfriend waiting for you downstairs, will you have dinner with me?"

Amie's heart pounded violently in surprise. "There's no boyfriend, but you've no need...I don't want..." She took a deep breath and started again. "Thank you for the invitation, but it isn't necessary, Liam. I agreed to work long hours when I took the job."

"But you didn't contract for slave labor," he said. "Anyway, my invitation was entirely selfish. I'm exhausted, Amie, and I don't feel like going home to an empty apartment and cooking my own dinner. Since my wife died—" He cut off his words abruptly. "I'd rather not eat alone," he said.

She knew she ought to refuse. She needed to get home to the lonely security of her apartment so she could decide what new approach her revenge against Liam would take. She reminded herself that she still hated him for ruining her life. She wasn't going to give up her plans just because her first scheme had proven impractical.

She turned toward him, ready to refuse his invitation. He was leaning against the desk, rifling through the computer printout sheets, and the bright desk lamp highlighted the lines of exhaustion that were etched onto his harsh features. She remembered that his day had started with a 6:00 A.M. site meeting, and her heart tightened with a reluctant twist of sympathy. His stance was deliberately casual, but she knew instinctively that her answer was important to him. For whatever reasons, he really wanted to have dinner with her. Her words of refusal died away unspoken.

"Thank you," she said slowly. "It *is* late, and I'm hungry too. If you'll just give me a couple of minutes to freshen up, I'd be happy to join you."

He looked up from the pile of printout sheets, and she saw that some of the tension was already gone from his face. "Thank you, Amie," he said quietly.

CHAPTER FOUR

SHE COMBED HER hair back from her face, pinning it securely so that no stray wisps could escape from her neat French plait, and put on some lipstick. A rush of dissatisfaction engulfed her as she surveyed her drab reflection in the mirror, but she reminded herself that she looked exactly the way she wanted to look—neat, competent, and thoroughly businesslike.

Liam was still reading her computer estimates when she came out of the washroom. "Ready?" he asked. "It's such a fine night, I thought we could walk to the restaurant."

She nodded her agreement, and his gaze raked over her as they waited for the elevator. "I liked your hair better before, when it was floating around your shoulders." He grinned with unexpected charm. "It looked very sexy that way. Both ethereal and sensuous at the same time."

"I have no desire to look sexy," Amie said, and even to her own ears the words sounded unbelievably prim. More important, she suddenly wasn't sure she was telling the truth.

"I can understand your feelings." Liam put his hand under her elbow as they crossed the street. "It's a real dilemma for an attractive professional woman, isn't it? If you make the most of your looks, people accuse you of sleeping your way to the top. If you try to downplay your natural attractions, people accuse you of denying your femininity in order to achieve success in a man's world."

She wondered if Liam could possibly be saying that he found her attractive, but she dismissed the thought immediately. She had seen some of the stunningly beautiful women he had escorted over the past few weeks, so she knew what high standards he was accustomed to. "I guess it's a problem that will only be solved when there are many more successful businesswomen," she said, hoping her voice sounded entirely impersonal. Why should she care whether or not Liam found her attractive?

"Probably," he agreed. "But I wish there was some other solution while we're waiting for all those competent women to make it to the top." He indicated a small sign, fifty yards ahead. "That's where we're going," he said. "Chez Jacques."

The restaurant was brightly lit and humming with a cheerful level of noise. The menu was scrawled on a chalkboard and there were no tablecloths, but as soon as she tasted the crisp, crusty bread and cold, fresh butter, Amie guessed that the food would be superb.

"Tell me something about yourself," Liam said when the waiter had taken their order. "I know you came to Chicago four years ago, but where are you from? Are your parents still living?"

Having expected some personal questions, she managed to meet his gaze with apparent openness. "I grew up in a small town in Missouri," she lied, "but Chicago seemed a better place to pursue my career once I finished college. It's a big city, but not too far from home."

"Your family didn't want you to move away?"

"Well, I guess my parents didn't mind much one way or the other. My parents and I weren't all that close. They're pretty much homebodies, and I'm not." The lies slipped easily from her tongue, carrying the ring of conviction because she had told them so many times during the past few years. She switched the conversation quickly and smoothly, another technique she had perfected since her trial. "What about you, Liam? Where are you from originally?"

For a split second there was a gleam in his eyes that made her afraid, but then he smiled so affably that she knew she must have imagined it. "I'm from New York," he said. "A true product of the inner city. I think I was fifteen or sixteen before I realized flowers didn't always grow in boxes and that leaves weren't always coated with a layer of gray grease."

"That's the exact opposite of my childhood," she said, forgetting for a moment to be properly cautious. "It wasn't until I made friends at college that I realized most people don't call a three-story building a highrise!"

He laughed with real amusement, and she discovered that she liked the sound of his warm laughter. "Where did you go to school, Amie? Where did you make your big discovery about highrises?"

She didn't want to say anything that would connect her with the southern part of Illinois. At all costs she must avoid any mention of the town of Riverside. He hadn't remembered who she was yet, but he surely would if she began giving him accurate clues about her background. Perhaps what she had already told him was too close to the truth. Maybe she should have said she was from California.

She took a sip of wine, swallowing it nervously. "I drove into St. Louis each day," she improvised quickly. "I attended a local community college there. What about you?"

She felt another moment of fear when his gaze seemed to flick over her with devastating penetration. But once again the ease of his manner dispelled the tension almost before she was aware of it. "I started out at the City College of New York," he said. "Fortunately they had an open-admissions policy or I'd never have made it off the streets and into the halls of academia." He grinned ruefully. "I wasn't what you'd call an enthusiastic student while I was in high school, but a couple of dedicated professors at City College persuaded me to make an effort. With their help I won a scholarship to graduate school, and when I had my M.B.A. I was hired by the federal government. About three years ago I started my own consulting firm, working mainly for private industry, but occasionally for the government as well."

She knew there were several questions she ought to ask, or he would wonder why she hadn't done so. Unfortunately, they were all questions she wanted to avoid. Liam's previous career was another of the topics too dangerous to discuss. She took a sip of water, grateful for its coolness on her tight throat. "What were you studying in graduate school?" she asked finally, hiding her reluctance as best she could. "What did you do when you were with the government?"

The tawny eyes found hers again before she could look away. "I thought the office rumor machine would have churned out all this basic information," he said. "I majored in advanced computer technologies and then worked as a special investigator in Washington. I was one of the Commerce Department's experts on detection of computer-related crime."

"H–how interesting."

"It was interesting at first, but I began to suffer from job burnout after a while. I started my own firm because I got tired of dealing with liars, cheats, and criminals. Too many shattered lives can become depressing."

Amie flinched. It was impossible to conceal her reaction to his words. She searched his face for some trace of hidden meaning, but she could find nothing. His features displayed only conventional politeness. She reassured herself that he was merely making small talk, but several moments passed before she recovered her voice. "It must have been difficult for you," was all she managed to say.

Liam nodded, giving no sign that he was aware of her constraint. "I was delighted to be offered the job with National Development because it gives me a chance to widen the scope of my day-to-day activities. But I think computer fraud is a fascinating subject, and I'm still interested in developing better methods to prevent it. Most companies rely on security systems that are way out of date, and they tend to protect themselves against the wrong sort of crime and the wrong sort of criminals. Employers don't like to admit that they're in danger of being ripped off by their most trusted employees. They prefer to pretend that all robberies are committed by armed lunatics carrying sawed-off shotguns. Banks and insurance companies are particularly vulnerable to employee fraud, and they're often the organizations that are least willing to take steps to protect themselves."

Once again Amie could think of absolutely nothing to say. She was grateful that the warm restaurant kept a flush of color on her pale cheeks. It was a great relief when she saw their waiter approaching. "Here comes dinner," she said with false heartiness. "Doesn't everything look good? My scallops smell delicious. I love seafood."

Liam accepted the change of topic with apparent willingness. He made a few polite remarks about the quality of their food, then switched to a discussion of her weekend activities. Without quite realizing how he had managed to draw her out, she found herself talking about her work at the center, describing some of the frustrations and pleasures of working with young blind people. "The basic problem is that there's never enough money," she said. "It's terrible when the director has to turn students away because he doesn't have the money to pay for an adequate teaching staff. Graduates of the center almost always become self-supporting, so it's a false economy to deny young students the training they need."

Liam agreed, and questioned her about the center's methods for raising funds. By the time the waiter arrived to remove their dinner plates, he had suggested several new sources of government and private funding that the director might want to consider. Amie was genuinely grateful for his interest and impressed by his knowledge in an area so far removed from his own special field.

When their coffee arrived, the conversation turned to the office, and they began to discuss the agenda for an upcoming sales meeting. Liam listened attentively to her suggestions, interrupting occasionally to ask questions that always seemed to stimulate a fresh flow of ideas. Amie slowly sipped her second cup of coffee and thought how efficiently they worked together and how much she was beginning to enjoy her job. It wasn't a thought that made her comfortable. However much she might have changed over the past four years, their earlier conversation showed that Liam's attitude toward liars, cheats, and criminals had not softened one bit since the day he'd arrested her. He would utterly despise her if he ever remembered the truth.

She accepted a liqueur from the waiter and glanced around the bistro to avoid Liam's eyes. Lord, but she wished she hadn't come tonight! She hated the strange restlessness that had invaded her body over the past few weeks, and tonight it was more acute than ever. She saw a pretty young woman enter the restaurant escorted by a man who looked like a candidate for the title of Mr. Universe. The woman's face lit up when she saw Liam. She murmured something to her escort and arrived at the table just as Liam looked up. He rose to his feet, smiling a welcome.

"Hello, friend," the woman said, her voice soft and full of husky laughter. "I've caught you out! You swore to me that you were going to Florida today, and instead I find you in Chicago, taking your date to *my* favorite restaurant!"

Amie felt her cheeks flush a brilliant, unbecoming red. She was aware of Liam's gaze resting speculatively on her before he smiled indulgently at the other woman.

"Hello, Laura," he said. "You're looking fabulous as always." He put his arm around her shoulders and pulled her close enough for a quick kiss on the cheek. "I *was* in Florida, and I got back less than two hours ago. This is a business dinner."

"Excuses, excuses!" Laura pouted prettily, then turned to Amie, her smile perfectly friendly. "You must be one of Liam's colleagues," she said. "I'm sorry if I've interrupted an important discussion."

"We were almost finished," Liam said. "By the way, Laura, I'd like you to meet my secretary, Amie Fletcher. Amie, this is Laura Wallace, a good friend of mine."

"Hello, Amie," Laura said, and there wasn't a trace of suspicion or envy in her voice. "I'm very pleased to meet you. How long have you been working for Liam?"

"About a month," Amie said, thinking how stiff and unattractive her voice sounded in comparison to Laura's. She stood up to shake hands and discovered she was at least four inches taller than the other woman. She felt sure she looked like a cross between a beanpole and a scarecrow next to Laura's exquisite, petite femininity. Looking at the soft, figure-hugging folds of the other woman's dress, Amie suddenly hated her own sensible gray skirt and white tailored blouse. "Liam has only been with National Development for a couple of months," she added stiltedly.

"Well, don't let him drive you too hard," Laura said. Her eyes twinkled with silent laughter as she peeped at Liam through her lashes. "I've always suspected he's a slave driver at the office."

Liam pretended to scowl. "I thought I could rely on you not to give away my secrets! Didn't you realize I was hoping my sins would go undetected?"

Amie sat down woodenly, listening to their banter, a smile frozen onto her face. She was piercingly aware of the admiration reflected in Liam's eyes, and Laura's sultry voice began to grate against her eardrums. She saw Liam glance toward Laura's escort and heard him murmur, "He looks like formidable competition. I think I'm jealous."

"I wish I believed that," Laura said. "But unfortunately there's no reason for anybody to be jealous. I was misguided enough to ask him how he keeps in shape, and he's been filling me in on the details of his program for the last hour and a half. So far he's only explained how he works on his biceps. I'm afraid to guess how long it's going to take to get all the way down to his toes! I don't know if I'll survive an entire evening of his conversation."

"I'm sure you'll find some way to stop him from talking," Liam said, but so softly that Amie was certain he hadn't intended for her to hear. "You'd better get back to him before he starts chewing the table. He's looking pretty frustrated."

"Why don't we join forces?" Laura suggested. "We have so much to talk about, Liam, and we always have such fun together."

"Liam and I have already eaten," Amie replied tightly. "I have a lot of work to get through tomorrow, and I think I should get home. But if you want to stay, Liam, I can easily call a cab."

Laura's glance rested for a moment on Amie's tightly coiled hair and drab clothes and the tiniest hint of scorn flashed in her eyes. "Couldn't you manage a late night, just for once?" she asked. "We could go dancing. A wonderful new nightclub just opened up on State Street."

Amie knew that Liam had turned to look at her, but she refused to meet his eyes. "Another night, Laura," she heard him say. "I was up at four-thirty this morning and I'm not in the mood for dancing. But I'll call you tomorrow and we'll set something up."

"I'll be waiting," she said softly. She held out her hand and took Amie's cold fingers in an apparently friendly clasp. "Good night," she said. "Don't let this workaholic keep you chained to your desk. Every woman is entitled to a *little* fun." She left their table with a cheerful good-bye and a last lingering look at Liam.

Liam settled the bill quickly and found a cab, insisting on escorting Amie home to Evanston. As soon as he had given directions to the driver, he leaned back against the worn leather seat, weariness showing in the slump of his shoulders. "Lord, I'm tired," he said. He closed his eyes and Amie felt a peculiar wrenching sensation when she saw how the lines of exhaustion had returned to his face.

"You shouldn't work so hard, Liam." The words flew out of her mouth almost before she knew she was thinking them. She immediately wished she could call them back. Liam opened his eyes and smiled wryly.

"I'm sorry if I'm not being very entertaining company. One way and another, it's been a hell of a day."

"You don't have to entertain me," she said shortly. "I'm your secretary, not Laura Wallace." She could have bitten her tongue off as soon as she had spoken. He looked at her intently, but before he could say anything the car drew to a halt outside her apartment house and she hurried out of the cab.

Liam said something to the driver, then strode quickly across the strip of pavement. He caught up with her in the apartment lobby. She turned and held out her hand.

"Thank you for a very enjoyable dinner," she said stiffly. "And thank you for seeing me home. Good night, Liam."

He gently pushed away her outstretched hand and reached up to touch her hair, his thumb pushing one loose strand behind her ear. His hands moved down the sides of her face to cup her chin, and he stood for a moment looking at her, his eyes very dark in the shadows of the doorway. She had the craziest impression that he was going to kiss her, and her eyes closed in restless anticipation. But instead, she felt the swift brush of his fingertips against her cheek, and then he was no longer near her. "Good night, Amie," he said as he turned toward the cab. "Sleep well."

By the time she reached her apartment she was furiously, almost uncontrollably angry. She stormed into her tiny bedroom, flinging her purse onto the bed and kicking off her plain low-heeled shoes. She tore at the pins holding her hair in place, not caring that they scattered over the floor as she shook her head violently to loosen the braids. Her hands shook as she ripped off her blouse and skirt. She threw the dowdy outfit carelessly toward a chair, missing her goal by at least a foot, but she didn't bother to pick anything up.

She walked across the room and flung open her closet so that she could see her reflection in the full-length mirror attached to the door. Even away from Laura's petite prettiness, she still looked like a beanpole, a beanpole with wild blond hair, wearing sensible white panties and a bra that was designed like a piece of armor plating. In the restaurant she must have looked every bit as dowdy as she did now, like a stereotyped spinster from a 1930's movie. A fresh burst of anger raged through her.

She was still wearing her glasses, and she reached up

slowly to remove them, rubbing the bridge of her nose where they had left little red marks on her skin. She couldn't bear to look in the mirror any longer, and she turned away to inspect the scanty contents of her wardrobe. She could find no reasonable excuse for the dreary gray-brown outfits that hung in a limp row.

With a fresh surge of angry energy, she pulled all her clothes out of the closet and tossed them onto her bed. She looked through the pile, but the search only made her angrier. How could she look beautiful in clothes like these? How could she make Liam see she was every bit as desirable as Laura Wallace when her wardrobe looked like something designed for an order of elderly nuns?

Amie sat down on the bed with a bump as she registered the significance of her thoughts. She pressed her fingers against her eyes, wondering if she had gone momentarily crazy. She sprang off the bed and began to return her outfits to the closet as fast as she could. There was no reason in the world why she should want to change her appearance.

She accidentally caught sight of herself in the mirror as she was returning the last skirt to the closet. She stared at her reflection, holding the skirt tightly against her body. It was made of a thin wool weave, more blue than gray, and she had never worn it to the office. Even on the hanger, its flared skirt fell in seductive swirls against her legs and its color emphasized the subtle glow of her eyes.

She turned her back on the mirror and hung the skirt over a chair, ready to wear the next morning. She hesitated for a moment and then, with a faint shrug, walked over to her chest of drawers and extracted a cotton-knit top from the stack of neatly folded blouses. It was nearly

summer, she reassured herself, and time she wore something with shorter sleeves and a lower neckline. She put
the top on the chair, next to the skirt.

She rummaged around in the back of the closet until
she found a pair of black high-heeled sandals that had
remained in their box for the last four years. She flexed
the soles, testing for cracks. The leather seemed to have
held up very well, and the style was surprisingly current.
She placed the shoes neatly alongside the chair. They
looked good next to the soft teal blue of the blouse and
skirt. Discreetly fashionable, she thought.

With quiet, controlled movements, she walked into
the bathroom and brushed her teeth. She rinsed her mouth
with ice-cold water and wondered if it was the frigid
temperature of the water that caused her to shiver.

She climbed into bed, pulling the covers up to her
chin. It was too late to start thinking up schemes for
revenge. She would get some sleep now and make plans
tomorrow, when she felt fresh. Tomorrow she would
have no difficulty in thinking of some way to get even
with Liam Kane. She was bound to find it an easy task
because she hated him. Of course she hated him. She
had hated him for four long years.

She reached up to turn off the light, and the blue skirt
and high-heeled sandals were the last things she saw
before darkness blanketed the bedroom. She wished they
hadn't been.

CHAPTER FIVE

NEXT MORNING, AMIE arrived at the office even earlier than usual. She scuttled through the empty lobby and entered the elevator, breathing a sigh of relief that she hadn't met anybody other than a security guard and a janitor. The muted blues of her skirt and blouse seemed to her to be as conspicuous as a a neon-light billboard, and she wanted to avoid the curious stares of her fellow workers. As she left the elevator on the twentieth floor, she tugged at the cotton knit of her skirt, but the soft fabric persisted in hugging the contours of her body. She should never have worn this outfit. She felt exposed, almost naked, like a caterpillar that had sloughed off its old skin before a new one was fully grown and now huddled in the grass, vulnerable to any keen-eyed bird.

She hesitated outside her office door, half inclined to

go home and change before Liam—before anybody—saw her. She touched her hair in a quick, nervous gesture. She had arranged the long, pale blond strands in a loose knot at the nape of her neck, secured only by tortoiseshell combs, and the knot felt as if it was about to fall down.

Forcing her thoughts away from useless worries about her appearance, Amie walked into the office as briskly as her high heels would permit. It was time she stopped asking herself so many soul-searching questions about what she was doing and why. She suspected she wouldn't like the answers anyway.

Early as it was, Liam had arrived before her. She could hear the quiet murmur of his voice in the inner office. She put her purse inside the closet, then leaned for a minute against the door, listening to him dictate a series of memos into his tape recorder. Unbidden, an image of the Riverside courtroom flashed into her mind, and she remembered how much she had once hated his crisp, controlled speech. Chills rippled down her spine, and she discovered she still had an intense reaction to the authoritative timbre of his voice. She silently admitted that she was frightened of Liam Kane's effect on her, although she had no logical reason to be afraid. There was nothing he could do to punish her even if he did discover the truth about her past. Nothing he could do, except perhaps despise her.

His dictation stopped so abruptly that she had no chance to move away before he entered her office. She had no hope of pretending to be busy. He stood in the doorway, not saying anything, simply looking at her in a way that made her pulse race and her body shiver.

"That's a very attractive outfit," he said at last, breaking the tense silence. "Is it new?"

"Yes . . . no . . . I haven't worn it to the office before. It's part of my summer wardrobe."

He smiled the warm smile that always twisted Amie's stomach. "Hooray for summer," he said. "I can tell it's going to be my favorite season." He walked casually toward her across the room. She pressed her hands tightly against the cool steel of the closet door and felt her heart begin to pound as she watched him approach. It was almost as if she were afraid of betraying some terrible secret if he came too close. Her body froze into a lump of chiseled ice when he reached up and gently removed her glasses. "You have beautiful eyes," he said. "Why do you hide them?"

"I'm nearsighted." It required phenomenal willpower to answer him normally.

"You could wear contacts."

"I prefer not to. Would you please give me back my glasses? We both have a lot of work to do this morning, and I'll need them."

His sigh was deliberately exaggerated. "Did anybody ever tell you you're a workaholic, Ms. Fletcher?"

She wouldn't look at his teasing smile; it was too dangerous. "No," she said. "My previous employers were always highly satisfied with my efforts on their behalf." The irony of her words suddenly struck her, making her blush with unwelcome memories of Jeff Cooper and how he had used her.

She turned away quickly, but not soon enough. "Amie, what is it?" The touch of Liam's fingers against her cheek seemed as tender as a lover's caress, and she felt an almost overwhelming urge to scream or cry or do something else equally melodramatic.

"Nothing's the matter," she said, jerking away from

his touch. "We have a lot of work to do, that's all." She started to push past him, intending to barricade herself behind her desk, but she forgot that a drawer in the file cabinet was still open. She caught her narrow heel in a loose thread of carpeting and stumbled awkwardly against the open drawer, banging her ribs with painful force. For a moment the pain was so sharp that she couldn't breathe.

Liam was quickly at her side. He took her into his arms, holding her in a gentle, comforting grip. She was intensely aware of his nearness, of the hard bone and muscle of his body as it pressed against her. His hand rested on her rib cage, just beneath her breast, and her heart throbbed against his fingertips. For one wild moment she wondered what it would feel like if his hand moved upward and caressed the gentle curve of her breast.

Shocked by the vividness of her thoughts, she immediately tried to move away. Liam's arms prevented her. Slowly but determinedly, he turned her around to face him.

"Are you all right?" he asked. His voice was low pitched, slightly strained.

"I'm fine."

"You're trembling."

"No . . . no, I'm not."

"You don't make a very convincing liar, Amie," he said huskily. He reached out and touched a strand of her pale blond hair. "You've lost your barrette. It must be somewhere on the floor."

"I'd better look for it before somebody steps on it. Would you let me go, please?" She could only speak coherently by exercising the utmost self-control. It was agony to be this close to the man she hated. That must be why her body refused to stop trembling.

"I'll let you go when you stop shaking," he said. His hand trailed softly, tantalizingly, down her spine, and she bit her lip in an effort to conceal her violent reaction to his touch. Did he know the effect he was having on her? Was that why he persisted in this subtle form of torture?

She told herself that in a minute she would walk away, that he couldn't prevent her, but the touch of his hand on her back made her legs shake even more than before, and she wasn't sure she could make it to her desk. Liam's fingers began to trace a delicate pattern on the nape of her neck underneath the heavy weight of her hair. "Won't you tell me why you're trembling, Amie?" he asked softly. "Tell me what's frightening you."

"I don't . . . I don't know."

He took her hand and held it against his chest so that she could feel the thud of his heartbeat racing beneath her palm. "Is it because you want the same thing I want?"

"No, I don't want anything! I mean, I don't know what you want."

"I'll give you a clue," he said, and he put his arms around her shoulders, pulling her close against his body. "I want this," he said, and his lips brushed over hers, cool and firm, then suddenly fierce and unexpectedly urgent.

She held her body ramrod stiff as her nebulous fears took instant shape and form. This, she realized, was what she had feared for the last five weeks. It was this quivering sensation of imminent discovery that she had dreaded experiencing with Liam Kane. She tried to turn her head away, but his tongue traced the soft outline of her lips, and her body shuddered with an irresistible wave of pleasure. She willed herself to resist the frightening, exquisite sensations that pounded on the edges of her consciousness, tempting her to collapse into his arms.

"Let me go," she said through clenched teeth.

"Not yet," he said. "You haven't kissed me."

"This isn't a game, Liam."

"Do you think I don't know that?" His words ended in a strange sound, half laughter, half groan. "Kiss me, Amie. Please kiss me."

Her heart thudded with a mixture of fear and desire as he leaned forward to trace a path of kisses from her cheek to her mouth. A tremor raced through his body when his lips finally covered hers, and then she had the strange sensation that she was melting into him, as if an electric current was dissolving her flesh and joining her irrevocably to Liam Kane. With the tiny, rational part of her mind that was still functioning, she tried to cling to the memory of all the bitterness and deception that lay between them, but the memory seemed faint, elusive, not worth pursuing. For a few panic-stricken moments there was no past, no future, no reality except Liam. He was the rock that kept her from being hurled away into a frightening new world of physical sensation. Her lips parted under his, and he kissed her deeply, hungrily, until she suddenly realized that he wasn't the rock but the ocean that threatened to drown her with the force of its waves.

She pulled her head back, dismayed at the effort of will required to break away from the kiss. "Stop it, please," she said. Her lips felt cold where she had turned away from him, as if they had been cut off from some vital source of energy or nourishment. She spoke with deliberate harshness, a harshness aimed at herself rather than

Liam. "I'm your secretary, not your mistress. Please remember that."

For a long moment he didn't answer, his eyes staring into hers; then his mouth twisted into a faint smile as he released her. "Any time you feel like taking on double duties, let me know. I'd be happy to pay overtime."

She didn't know why his cynical response caused a twist of pain somewhere in her midriff. She seemed to walk across acres of floor before she reached the sanctuary of her desk. "We have a busy schedule, Liam, as I tried to remind you earlier today. Are you ready to start work now?"

"Yes, certainly." His voice was at least as cool as her own. "Please bring your notebook into my office. I'd like you to sit in on the West Florida meetings. I'm not altogether happy with the way the project manager is handling the detailed survey of the site."

She picked up her notebook and a supply of sharp pencils. "Would you please give me back my glasses?" she said, hating the quaver in her voice. "I believe you still have them."

He picked up the glasses from the top of the file cabinet and handed them to her without comment. She put them on with almost feverish haste and twisted her hair back into as tight a knot as the combs would hold. Looking up she found that Liam was watching her. His face was set, his expression grim.

"Ms. Fletcher returns with a vengeance," he said. "I wish she hadn't. I think I would have enjoyed getting to know the real Amie." He turned abruptly, and when he spoke again his voice sounded as it usually did, casual and faintly mocking. "Let's get started," he said. "I wouldn't want to waste any more time on such a busy day. Find the Glencoe folder and bring it in, will you? There are a couple of problems cropping up in Florida that I think we've already solved in Glencoe."

She heard his instructions as if they were being issued by somebody speaking at a great distance. It was less than a minute since she had scraped back her hair and put on her glasses, but she knew with sudden blinding certainty that she didn't want to return to her role as the prim, dreary Ms. Fletcher. She wanted to become the real Amie, whoever that might be. She walked over to the file cabinets, dazed by the intensity of her feelings. "Did you say the Glencoe file?" she murmured. "I'll bring it right in."

They worked the rest of the day without referring to what had happened. Amie was on the point of leaving the office when she looked up to find Liam standing in front of her desk. "I've come to apologize," he said, before she could speak. "I've always despised men who take advantage of the closeness of a working relationship to force themselves on their female colleagues. I can assure you that a situation like this morning's won't occur again. It's one of my firmest rules never to mix my business and social lives."

"Is it?" She avoided his eyes, wondering why his words of reassurance didn't please her. "Thank you for the apology, Liam, but let's forget about this morning, all right? It was only a kiss. I'm twenty-six years old, and I have been kissed before."

"I know," he said. "I could tell."

She didn't realize what she was planning to do until she stopped at Marshall Field's on the way home that night. Going straight to the lingerie department, she by-passed the shelves stacked with "firm support foundation garments," where she usually bought her plain white panties and stiffly boned cotton bras. She finally stopped at a display of peach-colored wisps of lace, the fabric so transparent and skimpy that at a quick glance it was impossible to distinguish the bra from the bikini panties. She stared at the display for a considerable time without moving, then rifled along the rack until she found her size. She quickly removed a matching set and took it over to the check-out desk before she could change her mind.

The saleswoman was young and friendly. "These are real nice," she said. "They're the latest style; they just came in. We have the same set in black and beige if you're interested."

Amie drew in a deep breath. "Thank you. I'll take a set in each color."

The saleswoman added two wisps of black and two wisps of beige to the scraps of peach lace already in a bag on the counter, then swiftly rang up the sale. Amie's smile was somewhat strained as she picked up the package. It seemed very small to contain three complete sets of underwear.

"Have a nice evening," the saleswoman said.

"Yes, I'm sure I will. I'm going to buy a whole new summer wardrobe."

"Lucky you!"

The saleswoman's words rang in Amie's ears as she continued to tour the department store. By the time she arrived home, she had two big boxes full of new clothes and another two boxes containing shoes. She put the pile of parcels on the living-room sofa, then went straight to the kitchen and pulled a black plastic garbage bag from the dispenser pack under the sink. She hurried into her bedroom and flung open the closet doors, then swept all the drab gray outfits off the rail in one sweeping gesture and dumped them into the garbage bag. Finally she went over to her dresser and tossed all the sensible white cotton underwear on top of the skirts and blouses. The garbage bag was stuffed tight by the time she had finished. On Saturday, she would deposit the clothes at a Salvation Army pick-up center. They were of good quality and might be useful to somebody—a woman approaching her ninetieth birthday, perhaps.

She stood for a long time under a pounding shower before she went to bed, not really thinking about anything, just feeling the hot water as it ran over her body and curved around the swell of her breasts, trickling more slowly down her thighs. A wonderful new scheme for revenge against Liam Kane hovered at the edge of her mind, just out of reach, and the thought made her smile with anticipation. She was sure the details would come to her eventually, and in the meantime she was looking forward to tomorrow.

Amie was acutely aware of the stares and whispers that followed her progress through the lobby when she entered the corporate headquarters of National Development the next morning. A faint warmth covered her high cheekbones, and her whole body felt flushed with excitement. This is it! She was filled with a heady sensation of power, a premonition of success that she knew was not entirely rational. Today was the start of her new plan for revenge, and this one was going to work, she was sure of it. She stepped into the elevator and smiled a dazzling greeting at a pair of gaping vice-presidents. "Amie..." one of them said. "You are Amie, aren't you? Mr. Kane's secretary?"

"Yes, I'm Amie. How are you, Mr. Callahan?"

"Fine, fine. It's a fine morning, isn't it?"

She nodded politely, and nobody spoke again until the elevator halted at the executive floor. "Thank you," she said when Mr. Callahan stood aside to let her pass. She included both bemused vice-presidents in her parting smile. "Good morning, gentlemen," she said. "Have a good day." The cranberry-colored silk of her shirtsleeve just brushed Mr. Callahan's arm, and a gossamer cloud of perfume followed her from the elevator. Neither vice-president had managed to recover his voice by the time she entered her office and closed the door.

Liam was in her office, talking to one of the salesmen. His head jerked up at the sound of her entrance, and because she was looking at him so closely, she saw the emotion that flared for a split second in the depths of his eyes. But he controlled his expression almost at once, and his gaze became calculating as he swiftly assessed the details of her new appearance. She wished she knew what he thought of the softly draped hairstyle and delicate makeup, the low-cut silk blouse, the slender beige linen skirt, and the cranberry shoes which exactly matched her shirt.

She could only tolerate his silent inspection for a few seconds. "I'm sorry if I'm a little late," she said, hoping he would think her strange breathlessness was caused by rushing.

He accepted her apology with a quick nod. "You're not wearing your glasses," he said. "Have you forgotten them?"

"No." She wished he had said something quite different, something flattering, something that would show he had noticed she was a woman and not merely a human secretarial machine. "I decided I didn't need to wear them all the time," she said. "But I have them in my purse in case I start to get a headache." The telephone rang and she moved to answer it, aware that both men were watching her.

"It's for you, Liam," she said. "It's Mr. Ritters, the town councillor from West Florida. He says it's urgent."

"I'll take it in my office."

The salesman was still waiting when she finished putting through the call. "How are you, Doug?" she asked casually as she took the cover off her electric typewriter and began sorting through the stack of interoffice mail. "How's everything in sales these days? I hear the new secretary is wonderful."

"Er... yes, yes, wonderful. You're looking pretty good yourself, Amie. I scarcely recognized you. I guess working for Mr. Kane must agree with you."

"It has its moments," she agreed. "It's certainly never boring." She sat down at her desk and rolled a sheet of paper into the typewriter, but when she glanced up she saw that Doug was still standing close beside her. "Are you waiting to speak to Liam again?" she asked. "Didn't you finish your conference?"

"More or less," he said. "Actually, I was wondering if you would like to have lunch with me today. I could fill you in on what's been happening in the sales department since you left. We could talk over old times and everything."

"We didn't have any old times, Doug," she said gently. "I don't think..." The telephone console gave a little bleep to indicate that Liam had finished speaking, and she heard him slam the receiver into its cradle and approach the open doorway behind them.

Doug perched on her desk. "Don't say no, Amie. Please." It was obvious he hadn't realized Liam's telephone call was over. She looked up at him, making herself smile because she was quite sure Liam was watching her. She felt his eyes boring twin holes into her spine. How amazing it was that Doug could remain so oblivious to the tension Liam's presence generated. "You're very persuasive, Doug," she said, just as if she had no idea Liam was listening. "Thanks for the invitation. I'll enjoy having lunch with you. Does twelve-thirty sound okay?"

"Sounds great," he said. "Amie, I can't tell you—"

"Is there any possibility of discussing today's schedule of business meetings with you, Ms. Fletcher? If it doesn't interfere with the plans you're making for your social life, of course."

Doug jumped off the desk. "I'm sorry, sir," he said. "I didn't mean to interrupt Amie's work, but we're old friends."

"So I see." Liam's voice was devoid of emotion.

Amie stood up without any appearance of haste. She smiled brightly at Liam. "I didn't know you were through with your phone call," she said. "You should have let me know you were waiting for me, Liam. I'll bring in today's mail right away and the appointment schedule as well." She turned back to the young salesman, lowering her voice to a provocative huskiness. "And I'll look forward to lunch, Doug. Twelve-thirty."

Liam scarcely glanced at her when she walked into his office. He issued instructions with the same crisp courtesy that had marked their very early days together.

Only the faint compression of his mouth indicated to Amie that he was keeping his emotions—whatever they were—under tight control.

By mid-morning her nerves were starting to jangle every time he came near her. At midday he stopped by her desk with some papers he had signed and looked at her with the tense, narrow-eyed gaze he always adopted when he was assessing a particularly difficult problem. As far as Amie knew, it was the first time since early morning that he had bothered to look at her, and she ached to hear him make some complimentary remark. Didn't he realize why she had worn these clothes and cast off the disguise that had shielded her so effectively for the last four years? Didn't he realize it was for his sake that she had exposed herself so frighteningly to hurt and rejection?

She frowned, feeling nauseous. Good grief, what was she thinking! She hadn't changed her image for *Liam's* sake. She had changed it because of her new plan for revenge. She had woken up in the middle of the night and the whole plan had been there in her mind, fully formed as if she had worked out all the details while she slept. She wanted Liam to find her attractive, but not because she liked him. She was going to make him desire her, need her, maybe even love her, and then she was going to spurn him in a way that would humiliate him as thoroughly as she had been humiliated four years ago. She would make sure that he never again forgot Amie Fletcher.

The scheme had seemed nearly perfect last night because it involved only the two of them. She could hardly wait for the moment when Liam admitted that he wanted her and she coolly rejected him. Over the past few weeks the fact that he still didn't recognize her had gradually become intolerable to Amie. Had she really been so unimportant to him? Had her trial and near conviction been such an insignificant episode in his life?

"Why are you frowning?"

Liam's sharp question cut into her muddled thoughts. She had forgotten he was still standing on the other side of her desk. "There's no reason," she said, forcing her voice to sound casual. "I didn't even realize I was frowning."

"Do you need to wear your glasses? If so, for God's sake put them on, at least until you get yourself fitted with a pair of contact lenses. There's no point in giving yourself a headache."

"There's no problem," she repeated. "Thank you all the same, Liam."

He dropped a paperweight onto the documents he had just put on her desk. It landed with a distinct thud. "It's nearly lunchtime," he said. "I suppose you're still planning to keep that date?" She nodded. "Be sure you're back here by two," he said curtly. "I need you."

Amie tried hard to be friendly to the salesman over lunch at a nearby coffee shop, but her mind had little room to spare for exchanging pleasantries. Her efforts must have been reasonably successful, though, because as they were leaving, Doug reached across the table and took her hand. "Have dinner with me, Amie?" he asked.

She withdrew her hand gently, wondering why his touch aroused no reaction in her at all. Why didn't his fingers make heat flood under her skin and her stomach tighten with tension? "Thank you, Doug," she said. "But I can't have dinner with you. I'm busy tonight."

"And tomorrow night?"

"I'm afraid so."

Doug was silent for a minute; then he shrugged his shoulders philosophically. "I'll walk you back to the office," he said. "There's no point in making the big boss mad. I guess he can be pretty terrifying to work for. I sure wouldn't want to cross him."

"Oh no, you have the wrong impression," she said quickly, without stopping to think how strange it was that she should defend Liam. "He's extremely fair, and he's willing to help anybody who's prepared to work hard. Actually, I find him easy to please now that I understand his systems. He's a very considerate boss, and he always makes a point of thanking me when I've done the least extra thing. He's an incredibly brilliant man, you know. It's really enlightening to watch him work at close quarters."

She wondered why Doug's glance seemed somewhat wry. "I believe you," he said. "You're a persuasive witness."

It was late before she finished work that night. She was just putting a stray pen into her desk drawer, when Liam entered the room.

"I have to go to a board meeting next Monday in Connecticut," he said. "I've been asked to present a two-year strategic plan and a financial forecast to the directors of the parent company."

"Yes, I know," she said. "I've marked it in your calendar and in mine. Someone in the design department is already working on the slides for your presentation."

For the first time since she had taken the job as Liam's

secretary, she sensed a hint of uncertainty in his manner. His voice was quiet, almost hesitant, and he shoved his hands into the pockets of his slacks as if he didn't quite know what else to do with them.

"I would like you to come with me," he said at last. "This will be the first time I've met the full board of directors since I was appointed president, and I'd like to have you along. I'll be too busy answering questions and presenting facts to have time to take notes. Your help and your opinions would be invaluable to me."

She thrust away the irrational leap of excitement that raced through her. "I don't know, Liam," she said. "You never suggested that I might have to travel with you. I'm not equipped to take off from Chicago at a moment's notice. I'm not used to traveling."

His mouth tightened. "I'm not planning to leave until the weekend," he said. "I really need you with me on this trip, Amie."

"You're leaving on the weekend?" she asked. "We'd be spending the weekend together?"

"Only part of it," he said. "And it's strictly a working trip. I've told you already that I don't believe in mixing business and pleasure. The meeting is at nine o'clock on Monday morning, and because of the time difference I'll have to leave O'Hare on Sunday in order to get to Connecticut in time." He turned impatiently. "But you know all this, Amie. If it's the thought of sacrificing part of your weekend that's bothering you, I'll be happy to give you the following Friday off as compensation."

Goose bumps erupted on her arms when he finished speaking. This was the second time he had walked straight into a trap she was laying for him, and her success seemed too easy—frighteningly easy, in fact. Common sense suggested she should jump at the chance he was offering her. If she couldn't create a suitable opportunity to seduce Liam when they were away together for a weekend, then she would never be able to do it. But it was too soon. She wasn't ready for this. Her stomach was knotted with fear, not triumph. It had been almost too late when she discovered the weakness in her previous plan for revenge. What if her new plan had some equally fatal flaw that would only become apparent when it was too late to draw back?

"Amie, why are you taking so long to answer a simple question, for God's sake? I'm not asking you to prepare for a ten-year voyage to Mars. I'm giving you three days' warning, and all you have to do is pack an overnight bag and book a plane ticket."

"And an extra hotel room." The words were out before she could stop them. In view of her plans, they were particularly irrational.

"And an extra hotel room, of course," he agreed coldly.

"Well, all right then, If you really think you'll need me, I'll come. What time should I be at the airport on Sunday?"

"I'll pick you up at your apartment at seven in the morning, if you don't mind. I want to take the first flight out of O'Hare."

She didn't ask why he needed to leave so early when the board meeting wasn't until Monday morning. At that moment it seemed wiser to concentrate on getting home, where she could sort out her feelings. Discarding her disguise was proving a great deal more complicated than she'd anticipated. She comforted herself with the knowl-

edge that there were still three more days before Sunday.
Three days to think of all the good reasons why she
shouldn't accompany Liam Kane on a trip to Connecticut.

"Seven o'clock?" she murmured when she finally realized he was still waiting for her answer. "All right,
Liam. I'll be ready."

CHAPTER SIX

THEY PICKED UP a rental car at New York's La Guardia airport and drove across the Whitestone Bridge toward southern Connecticut. Amie found the noise and volume of the traffic on the New York Thruway bewildering, and the aggression of the drivers simply terrifying. "Couldn't all these cab drivers find an easier way to commit suicide?" she muttered as Liam successfully dodged yet another swooping attack by a lane-switching taxi.

He grinned. "It's tough making a living as a cabbie in New York. The drivers don't have time to watch out for the faint-hearted."

"Nobody faint-hearted could possibly drive through this open-air madhouse," she retorted. "Nobody sane would even try it." She watched in tense silence as Liam edged their Buick Regal into the flow of tightly jammed vehicles speeding off the bridge. As far as she could see, there was never more than half an inch between their car and the cars surrounding them. Liam leaned over and patted her hand. "Relax, Amie. I'm not going to have an accident. I learned to drive on these roads when I was in high school."

His hand remained curled over hers, warm and comforting. "Don't you need two hands on the wheel?" she said.

He grinned. "No. I learned to drive one-handed long before I passed driver's ed. I may have flunked math, English and social studies, but I was a whiz at all the extracurricular activities."

"I bet you were," Amie said, but she smiled as she replaced his hand on the wheel. "This road's very crowded," she commented. "Has *everybody* in New York decided to drive to Connecticut? Where do you think all these people are going at this hour on a Sunday morning?"

Liam chuckled with amusement. "To church, I guess. Or on a picnic, or to the beach, or maybe to visit friends. What nefarious purpose do you think they have in mind? These people pursue all the usual, humdrum human occupations, you know, even if they are New Yorkers."

"That's debatable," she said. "I don't think anybody has convincingly proven that New Yorkers are just normal human beings."

Liam threw back his head and laughed. "You must have forgotten you're speaking to a genuine New York City boy, born and raised. And I promise I'm human all the way through. No strange mental quirks and no mechanical parts, I swear it."

"None at all? Not even a few silicone chips to increase

your brain power? No implanted brass knuckles?" She turned to look at him and found his eyes gleaming with a golden sheen of laughter, and her heart began to pound erratically. "How far away is Stamford?" she asked quickly.

"About another fifteen miles to the center of town where all the corporate offices are, but we're going to stay a few miles beyond the town center. Is this your first trip to the New York area?"

"Not only my first, but very probably my last."

"You can't possibly mean that. New York's a fabulous city and you'd enjoy a vacation here. Although I'm discovering that Chicago has its own charms."

"To a native midwesterner, Liam, that faint praise sounded more than a bit patronizing. You ought to practice sounding a little more sincere."

"But I am sincere!" He sighed. "You country folks never give us city slickers a fair shake."

"My heart bleeds," she said dryly.

"It should." He glanced out of the window. "Stamford's two more exits. I guess you've never been to Connecticut either?"

"No," she admitted. "I've never been anywhere on the East Coast except Florida, to change planes. I really haven't traveled since Jef... since I arrived in Chicago. I mean, since I left home. Since I left my parents."

She knew she was babbling, but she was appalled at how close she had come to mentioning Jeff Cooper's name. She clamped her lips tightly together and turned away to stare unseeingly at the passing scenery.

Liam seemed unaware of her sudden tension. "Well, you'll probably have plenty of chances to travel in the future," he said casually. "Since you've never been in this area, would you like to take a drive into the countryside this afternoon?"

"But I thought . . . I assumed you would have work to do this afternoon."

"I have nothing to do that can't wait until we get back to the office on Tuesday."

"Don't you still have work to do on your presentation? I thought that must be why you wanted to leave Chicago so early this morning."

"No."

Amie turned away again, not wanting to risk another encounter with his tawny eyes. She told herself that it was past time she learned how to control the crazy breathlessness that grabbed at her throat every time Liam made a faintly suggestive comment. After all, what had he said except that he didn't have any urgent work to do? She tried hard to think of some noncommittal response to make, something that would start the conversation flowing again. "The countryside around here is really hilly," she said finally. "It's very different from the flat farmland of the area where I was raised."

"Yes, it is." She was grateful that his manner contained no hint of mockery at her trite remark. "We take the next exit," he added. "We turn off the Thruway at the toll booth here, and once we're on the side roads you'll see that the houses look a little different as well as the landscape. Even the newly built homes aren't quite the same as their counterparts near Chicago."

"It's pretty," she said, glancing around with real pleasure as they drove along a well-kept suburban road. "Some of these houses look very old. Do you think they're genuine Colonial survivors?"

"Could be," he said, "but I doubt it. There are quite

a few houses in Connecticut that date from the seventeenth and eighteenth centuries, but not many in this particular area. However, the hotel I asked you to book for us is one of the genuine old ones. It was built nearly two hundred years ago."

"As an inn?" she asked.

"Yes, it was one of the earliest in the region. The present owners are remotely related by marriage to the Tuckett family, the original owners, and they've done a terrific job of upgrading the plumbing and the electric wiring without ruining the Colonial atmosphere. You can take a hot shower *and* sleep in a solid maple four-poster."

"I hope the antique beds aren't too authentic," she said. "I'm not wild about nineteenth-century straw mattresses."

"No straw," he said. "I guarantee it." He turned the car into a winding lane that dead-ended at the entrance to a large New England frame house with narrow sash windows and two tall stack chimneys at either end.

"It looks too picture perfect to be real," Amie said. "There are even roses blooming around the front door, and it's only the beginning of June."

"I've asked the owners what their secret is, but they won't tell. The southern exposure may help." While he was talking, Liam took their overnight bags from the trunk of the car and walked toward the front door of the inn. "They don't serve meals here, except breakfast, so let's get signed in and then we can go for that drive. I'd like to revisit my old university campus—it happens to be in Connecticut—and I think you'd enjoy a tour."

Amie unpacked her suitcase quickly and took a hasty shower, since the plane ride had left her feeling grubby.

She had packed more clothes than she needed, partly because it felt so good to have so many attractive new outfits hanging in her closet, just waiting to be worn. After selecting a sapphire-blue skirt and a low-cut white blouse, she renewed her makeup and twisted her hair into a high, loose knot on top of her head.

There was an old-fashioned swinging cheval glass in her room, and when she caught sight of herself in it, she was frightened by the glittering shine of excitement in her eyes. She rummaged around in her bag and found a pair of sunglasses. She put them on with a sigh of relief, glad that the brilliant sunshine gave her an excuse to conceal eyes that she suspected revealed far more than she wanted them to. Liam knocked on her door just as she finished spraying perfume onto her arms and throat.

His eyes narrowed when she answered the door, but it was impossible to guess what he was thinking. "Ready?" he asked politely. "Like the room?"

She nodded, not trusting herself to speak. His hair was wet from a shower, and he had changed into a dark green knit shirt. He hadn't bothered to close any of the shirt buttons, and she discovered that her palms were sweaty when she picked up her purse from the bed. She pulled some tissues from the box on the nightstand and surreptitiously wiped her hands. Lord, her reactions were becoming more ridiculous by the minute! This was the same man she had worked with almost every day for the past five weeks. He was her worst enemy, for heaven's sake! She turned around, pasting a smile firmly on her lips. "Let's go!" she said brightly.

They didn't talk much at first. Liam was strangely silent as they got into the car, not teasing her as he had earlier in the day, and his mouth seemed drawn into a grim line. "Do you want to stop for lunch?" he asked after they had been driving for about twenty minutes.

"Not particularly. I had orange juice and cereal before I left home this morning, and then I had another breakfast on the plane. What about you?"

"I'm just as happy to wait for dinner." They continued their silent drive until Liam finally said, "We're here. I thought you might find Yale an enjoyable place to spend the afternoon."

She turned slowly to face him. "Yale University. *This* is what you meant when you said you would give me a tour of your old college campus? Do you mean that you won a scholarship to attend graduate school at *Yale?*"

He shrugged. "I told you there were a couple of outstanding professors at City College. They changed my perspective on the world. I guess they made me realize that there are more things in life than getting a place on a pro basketball team and making out with a different girl every night."

"You wanted to be a professional basketball player?" she asked, intrigued by this insight into the ambitions of a much younger Liam Kane.

"Honey, every kid in my neighborhood wanted to be a professional basketball player. There was nobody around our housing project to tell us that there are a thousand easier ways to get out of the South Bronx than via the basketball court."

"I didn't know anybody still lived in the South Bronx. I thought it was more or less a ruin."

"There are still a few habitable areas," he said tersely. "Depending on what you mean by habitable, I guess." He pulled the car into the visitors' parking area and got out of the car. "Let's walk around a little," he said, firmly changing the subject. "It's a glorious day for a tour."

The university campus was built around a handsome green at the center of the town of New Haven. As they strolled along the paths, Amie tried to imagine how the peaceful New England town with its graceful gothic buildings must have struck a young man whose horizons had previously been bounded by a graffiti-covered urban slum. In comparison to the economic and social deprivations Liam had suffered, the limitations of her own childhood suddenly seemed to be nothing more than the enviable limits imposed by her family's need to protect her.

"How long has Yale been in existence?" she asked, wanting to start some conversation—any conversation—to ease the growing sense of strain she felt in the silence between them. "I know it was going strong long before the Revolution."

"It was chartered as a collegiate school in 1701," Liam replied, as if reciting from a well-remembered tourist brochure. "The university library is one of the largest in the country and considered one of the finest. Probably only Harvard's can hope to be compared to it. The Peabody Museum of Natural History also has an outstanding reputation."

"What's that impressive gothic tower?" Amie asked. Sensing that he was lost in thoughts that totally excluded her, she walked a safe distance away from him, excruciatingly aware of the present moment. She had to hold herself very erect and stiff so that she wouldn't give in to the temptation to walk around campus clinging to his arm like a besotted eighteen-year-old in the throes of first love. She tensed even more at the involuntary mental image. She had already experienced the so-called joys of first love with Jeff Cooper, and she had no desire to repeat the experience with anybody, least of all with the man who had ruined her life.

"It's Harkness Tower," Liam said finally, still sounding like an official tour guide. "It's one of the more notable pieces of fake gothic architecture on the East Coast." They had reached a stretch of smooth, deserted lawn, and he stopped abruptly. "Mind if we sit here for a few minutes?" he asked. When she nodded, he flung himself down on the grass, pulling up a blade and chewing on its white tip.

"I haven't been back here for ten years," he said. He pulled at another strand of grass and shredded it into narrow strips. "I met Jackie here—my wife."

Amie's hand hovered over the bright yellow dandelion she had been about to pick, then went still. "Was your... was Jackie a computer scientist too?"

There was a long pause. "No," he said at last. "Jackie was a drama student. She won a place with England's Royal Shakespeare Company, but she gave it up to marry me."

"I'm sorry, Liam. You mentioned once how... how lonely you've felt since she died."

"She's been dead for four years," he said. "We only had two years together before she got sick. I guess the office grapevine filled you in on all the gory details."

"No," she said. "But I knew... I knew she died after a long illness."

He didn't say anything for a long while. He pulled up a few more blades of grass and took an inordinate amount of time braiding them together. He didn't look at her when he spoke again. "She was in such pain," he said. "She had shiny black curls that used to bounce around when she was excited, and when they started chemotherapy all her hair fell out except for a little wiry fringe at the nape of her neck." He pressed his hand against his eyes as if to block out an intolerable mental picture. "She was so frail, so tiny. At the end it seemed as if there wasn't enough space left in her arms for all the tubes they were trying to push into her."

Amie felt the blood draining from her face, and she quickly looked down, although she was sure Liam's thoughts were lightyears away from her and her reactions. This, she realized, was the personal hell he had been suffering when he was assigned to investigate the fraud case in Riverside. "I'm sorry, Liam," she said, not knowing if she was apologizing for the terrible indifference she had once shown to his problems or if she was simply aching with shared pain. "I'm so sorry."

He looked at her then, and a faint frown creased his forehead as he visibly jerked his thoughts back to the present. "It's all over now," he said. "I've accepted that you can't change the past; you simply learn how to live with it. Nowadays I mostly just remember the good times." He suddenly leaned over and took off her sunglasses, touching the tip of his finger to her wet cheeks. "Hey, what's this?" he asked, his voice gentle but teasing. "I thought I could rely on the stern Ms. Fletcher to help me keep my sense of perspective, and here you are crying. You're not allowed to be sentimental, you know. I'm quite sure it's against company regulations—and, anyway, it ruins your corporate image."

Amie scrubbed her cheeks with a tissue. "The cool, unflappable, unfeeling Ms. Fletcher," she said bitterly. "Is that the corporate image you're talking about, Liam? Don't you know stern spinsters always have melting hearts underneath their granite exteriors? It's a cliché from every Hollywood romance ever filmed."

He stared at her intently. "Amie . . ." he said huskily,

"I don't want it to be this way between us. I think you should know..."

Her lungs felt as though they couldn't draw in any air. "Yes?" she said. "What should I know?"

"I shouldn't have brought you with me today," he said. The pause before he spoke had been infinitesimal, but Amie felt sure he had hesitated on the brink of saying something completely different. For an insane moment she thought he was going to admit that he recognized her, that he had known all along who Amie Fletcher really was, and that he remembered what had happened in Riverside four years earlier. For an even more insane moment she actually wanted him to fling the accusation at her so that all the lies between them would be over and they could start fresh.

She took her sunglasses from him and put them on, taking refuge behind their comforting darkness. It would be easier to say what she was feeling if she knew Liam couldn't see her clearly. "I'm glad you asked me to come with you," she said. "I'm glad you didn't come back to the campus alone."

He touched her hand very lightly. "Nevertheless, Amie, I apologize for dragging you around when I decided to exorcise some rather painful ghosts."

She shook her head, forcing a smile that she hoped was casual enough to disguise the trip-hammer beat of her heart. "All part of the Fletcher secretarial service," she said, wondering if he could feel how her hand was burning beneath his touch. "I could use a long, cool drink," she added. "Do they sell iced tea in these exalted halls of learning?"

"They sure do," he said, accepting her change of subject without comment. He pulled her to her feet, then moved away so that there was no longer any point of physical contact between them. Amie told herself she was glad. She was certainly relieved to see that the terrible bleakness had finally gone from his eyes. "When we've had a drink, I think a tour of the Yale Art Gallery is called for," he said. "It houses yet another of the university's well-known and superb collections. I'm sure you'll be impressed."

"Yes," she said, "I'd like to see it. I seem to remember hearing that Yale has a large collection of Impressionist paintings."

"Are you a connoisseur?"

She looked at him, with the hint of a smile softening her lips. "Well, I'm working at it. Last fall I enrolled in a course of lectures at the Chicago Art Institute, but I came to the conclusion that I needed more than six lessons to understand the theory of modern art."

He grinned. "It was your first-ever art course?"

"Yes."

"Well, you're six lessons more of an expert than I am! I'm relying on you to see that I don't do anything dreadfully gauche like confusing a Manet with a Monet."

"It's a deal."

He kept the conversation light and impersonal while they drank tea at a small snack bar. They were strolling back along the path leading to the Art Gallery when he put out his arm and turned her around to face him, holding her loosely in his arms. He brushed his hand along her jaw, tipping up her chin to drop a tiny kiss on the corner of her mouth.

"Thank you for the tears," he said.

It was after six when he left her at the door to her room. "Our dinner reservations are for seven-thirty," he said. "Can you be ready in an hour?"

"Yes." She hesitated in the doorway. "Liam . . . you don't have to take me out tonight. I'd be perfectly content to call the local pizza parlor and ask them to deliver something."

"I want you to have dinner with me. Please."

"Well, all right. Thank you."

She showered and dressed with particular care, spending a long time on her makeup, even though she used only a little. The early summer sun had touched her face with subtle color and her eyes seemed to glow with new brilliance. She enjoyed the soft rustle of silk as her new black dress slid into place over her slender hips, the chiffon skirt drifting around her knees. She was just trying to tighten the strap on one of her evening sandals when there was a knock at the door.

She opened it, the sandal still clutched in her hand. She and Liam stared at each other, neither of them speaking. He was dressed in a dark gray formal suit with a white shirt and a conservatively striped tie. He looked the picture of a powerful, self-confident executive, and she thought with fleeting regret that there seemed nothing left of the vulnerable man with whom she had shared the afternoon.

She gestured with her shoe, feeling as bereft of poise as a sixteen-year-old on her first date. "Do you . . . would you like to come in?" she asked. "I'll only be a minute."

"There's no rush." Liam ushered her back into the bedroom, the punctilious courtesy of his manner emphasizing the barriers between them. "May I?" he asked, reaching out and taking her shoe. "If you'll sit up on the bed, I can fix this buckle." He slipped on the shoe, running his hand lightly over her instep. Her stomach

muscles clenched in unwilling reaction to his touch as
he tightened the strap around her heel. His expression
revealed none of the heightened awareness she herself
was feeling.

"Thank you," she said as soon as the catch was fas-
tened. She jumped quickly from the bed and smoothed
her skirt nervously. "I hope I'm appropriately dressed.
You didn't say where we were going."

"We're going to a restaurant about twelve miles from
here called The River Mill. The food's quite good, but
I really chose it because of the setting, which is sensa-
tional. The dining room's built around a waterfall. It's
illuminated at night and very attractive."

She had wanted him to say, "Amie, I think you look
beautiful," but instead he had recited the facts about their
destination in a flat monotone. She stole a covert glance
in his direction and saw that his expression was tautly
controlled, the line of his mouth drawn tight. She sighed,
not quite knowing why, and picked up her purse along
with the jacket that matched her dress. "I'm ready," she
said, and she was glad to realize that her voice contained
no more emotion than his.

The restaurant was as attractive as Liam had promised.
The hostess led them to a secluded table set into a bay
window that overlooked the waterfall, and Amie forgot
the tension that had built up during their drive as she
gave Liam a smile of genuine pleasure. They ordered
salads and a bottle of California Chablis, delaying their
choice of entree as they laughed together at the antics of
a family of ducks cavorting in a shallow pool at the foot
of the waterfall.

As she ate her salad, Amie gradually allowed herself

to relax. Just for tonight it wouldn't matter if she forgot the past. Right at this moment the fact that she had betrayed her family's dreams and unwittingly helped to defraud hundreds of innocent people didn't seem very important. She didn't even care that Liam Kane was her enemy, the man who had done his best to send her to jail. Her arrest and trial seemed to have happened a long time ago to a totally different Amie Fletcher. Perhaps after four years of penance she had earned the right to forgive herself.

She picked up her wineglass and took a sip of Chablis, glancing at Liam as she did so. He was watching the ducks turn their tails up in search of some tasty water bug for dinner, and the sternness of his mouth had relaxed into a faint smile. He turned unexpectedly and their eyes met. She felt the all-too-familiar knot form inside her stomach, and her pulse began to race with feverish rhythm.

Neither of them spoke for a long time, and when he finally broke the silence he didn't meet her eyes. "You're beautiful tonight, Amie," he said. "Stunningly beautiful."

She set her glass of wine on the table and placed her trembling hands in her lap, where they were hidden by the long white cloth. "Thank you," she said.

A waiter arrived at that moment to take their dinner orders. "I recommend the lobster thermidor," Liam said calmly, just as if they had spent the previous ten minutes discussing the menu. "I know you like seafood."

"Er . . . yes, thank you. I'll take the lobster."

She was surprised that Liam remembered what she had ordered on the only other occasion they had eaten dinner together. But then, she reminded herself, he had been trained for years to observe and remember precisely that sort of tiny detail. She felt a spurt of irrational anger and her fingers tightened around the table napkin that rested on her lap. She knew from her experiences four years ago as well as from her work as his secretary that his memory was phenomenal. Why, then, didn't he remember her? When she had sat in the Riverside courtroom, cringing under the ruthless inspection of his cold tawny eyes, hadn't he actually been seeing her?

The waiter added chilled wine to their glasses and put a loaf of fresh hot bread on the table. When he left, Liam leaned back in his chair, staring at her with a strangely quizzical expression. She wondered what he would say if he could look into her head and see the questions pounding in her brain. *Look at me,* she screamed silently. *Look at me, damn you, and remember who I am!*

For a split second she wondered if she had actually spoken. His eyes darkened with the dreadful bleakness she had seen that afternoon; then he dropped his gaze and emptied his wineglass with a single swallow. When he looked up again, his expression had changed completely and his smile held all the charm that routinely melted the female hearts at the National Development Corporation. "I've just made a rapid mental calculation," he said, and it seemed to Amie that a thread of genuine amusement now warmed his voice. "I estimate that we've spent nearly three hundred hours together and the only thing I know about your personal tastes is that you enjoy eating seafood. Tell me what you like doing in your spare time."

"For the last five weeks I haven't had any spare time," she said. "I've spent the weekends doing household chores and the week nights trying desperately to catch up on my sleep."

He smiled at her answer, his lean, strong fingers making patterns in the moisture that had condensed on his glass of water. "That, my dear Amie, wasn't a very subtle complaint. Are you by any chance trying to tell me something about your working conditions?"

"It was so clever of you to guess," she murmured, managing to produce a casual smile even though she really wanted to reach out and close her hand around his fingers, to feel their hardness against her soft palm.

"You should tell me frankly, Amie, if I'm working you too hard."

"No, no you're not," she said. "I . . . like working for you. I think we work well together."

The waiter returned with two platters of lobster in a delicate cheese sauce. "Enjoy your meals," he said as he set the dishes down with a flourish.

Amie dutifully swallowed a few mouthfuls of food. Apart from the preliminary salad, she had eaten nothing since breakfast, but her appetite was nonexistent. "It's very good," she said politely. "Yours, too?"

"Yes, it is. The owners of this restaurant fly the lobsters in directly from Maine, so they're always fresh. A great many restaurants in the Chicago area use frozen seafood, and I think you can taste the difference."

"Yes, I guess you can. The sauce is excellent, too." She swallowed a few more pieces of tender lobster, fighting against an hysterical desire to burst out laughing. Here they sat, solemnly chewing and discussing the relative merits of fresh fish, when what she really wanted to do—what she really ached to do—was . . . Her thoughts stumbled to an uneasy halt. She didn't want to think about what her real wants and needs might be.

She felt Liam's gaze fixed on her with unexpected

intensity, and she looked up quickly. The superficial charm had completely vanished from his eyes. "They have a little dance floor in the bar," he said. "Will you dance with me before we order dessert?"

"Yes, please," she said, without stopping to consider her reply.

He escorted her into the darkened cocktail lounge, his hand resting lightly on her back. The drumbeat of a four-piece rock band became much louder as they entered the bar and walked onto the polished hardwood floor. There wasn't much space for dancing, and Liam pulled her into his arms, trapping her hands inside his jacket against his crisp shirt. His arms held her tightly in a world in which there was only the two of them, alone with the music and the darkness.

Her body stiffened as his hands slid down her back to rest on the swell of her hips. She was intensely aware of his thighs moving against her as he guided her through the motions of the dance, and she had to struggle to prevent herself from arching her body more closely against him. As his fingers brushed lightly over her hair, she finally abandoned her useless efforts at self-deception and admitted to herself that Liam attracted her physically with an intensity that was too great to resist. With a sigh of resignation, she allowed her head to rest against his chest, drawing strange comfort from feeling his solid muscles beneath her cheek. It was amazing that during all the months she had imagined herself in love with Jeff, she had never yearned for his lovemaking, never ached with the need to be held in his arms. But Liam had only to touch her—sometimes only to look at her—and her body responded with all the symptoms of acute sexual desire.

The music stopped and she turned away, anxious to

return to the relative safety of their table, but he put out his arm and prevented her from leaving. "One more dance," he said softly. She pretended to hesitate, but it was a futile gesture. She could no longer deny the true significance of her shaking legs and pounding heart. She wanted Liam to hold her. More than that, she wanted him to make love to her, and the need was beginning to consume her.

He guided her away from the center of the small floor and into the darkness of a corner somewhat removed from the other couples. He held her close against his body with one hand, then put his other hand under her chin, tilting her face so that her mouth was only a breath away from his. He looked at her for a long time. "I want to kiss you," he said at last.

Without speaking, she met his gaze directly, no longer trying to disguise her feelings. She saw the sudden blaze of anticipation in his eyes and parted her lips in a silent, explicit invitation.

He grasped her shoulders and drew her closer. She heard the harshness of his indrawn breath just before he brushed his lips across hers in a brief, hard kiss. There was scarcely time for her to respond. The kiss was over far too quickly, and Liam relaxed his hold on her, putting some distance between them. "Don't look at me like that," he said curtly.

She veiled her eyes with her lashes. "Why not?"

"Because when you look at me like that I want to kiss you. And if I kiss you again, I may not be able to stop." His expression seemed forbidding in the semi-darkness, but she thought she could detect a trace of self-mockery in the clipped words.

"I . . . didn't ask you to stop," she said huskily. "Don't you find me . . . desirable?"

"You know damn well I find you desirable." He dropped his hands to her hips and pulled her angrily against his thighs. "You know what you're doing to me; you can feel it. But I'm too old to enjoy sneaking casual kisses on a dance floor, Amie. By the time I reached my eighteenth birthday that no longer seemed like a good way to spend my time."

"Do you want to make love to me, Liam?" she asked softly.

"Yes."

She reached up and touched her hand to his mouth. "Kiss me," she whispered.

For a moment she thought he was going to refuse; then his teeth bit into the soft ball of her thumb. "I must be crazy to do this." His words were a shaky murmur against her lips, but she paid scarcely any attention to them. She could feel the roar of her own blood pounding in her ears as Liam's mouth trailed a burning path of kisses from her throat to her lips. When his mouth finally covered hers, his kiss was hard and hungry. Then his lips softened and his tongue pushed gently against her mouth, coaxing her to respond. She needed no persuasion. She parted her lips willingly, shuddering with a strange, sweet pleasure when his tongue flicked against hers. She gave up all pretense of dancing, and the heavy beat of the music faded away from her consciousness until all she could hear was the throb of her heart, beating in unison with Liam's, and all she could see was darkness. For as long as he kissed her, there was no dance floor, no bartender, no couples dancing. There was nothing but the heat of his skin against her breasts and the cool enticement of his mouth moving over hers.

She was dazed when he finally drew away from her. "Let's get out of here," he said harshly.

She looked at Liam without seeing him. She didn't seem able to bring herself back to a universe that contained other things besides the two of them. She tried to speak but found she had forgotten how to string words together to make coherent sentences. Her body swayed closer to his, instinctively seeking support.

His arms tightened around her; then he put his hand under her elbow and guided her swiftly through the dimly lit bar. They walked along a short, narrow corridor and emerged through a heavy fire door onto a grassy area at the edge of the parking lot. The night air chilled her after the overheated bar, and Amie shivered, hugging her arms around her body.

Liam took off his jacket and silently draped it over her shoulders. He turned away, staring across the parking lot toward the waterfall.

"I'm sorry," he said after several moments of tense silence. "I shouldn't have hustled you off the dance floor like that." He shoved his hands into the pockets of his trousers, and his voice was full of mockery when he spoke again. "I had to get out of there because I was in danger of making a complete fool of myself. Social conventions may have changed a lot in the last few years, but I guess a full-scale seduction is still a bit more than most restaurants are prepared to tolerate."

His jacket didn't seem to be stopping her shivers. "Why won't you look at me, Liam?" she asked.

He turned around slowly, still not meeting her eyes. "Because I find you intensely desirable, and I'm trying hard to get my feelings for you under some sort of acceptable control."

."Acceptable to whom?" she asked. She looked down at her tightly clenched hands. "I didn't ask you to stop kissing me."

"I know. But you're my secretary, Amie, and I think our relationship is complex enough without adding this sort of dimension to it." Before she could ask him exactly what he meant, he reached out and gently tucked a loose strand of hair behind her ear. He sighed. "Just this once I want to say to hell with ethics. Have you any idea how beautiful you look tonight, Amie? Do you realize how much I want you?"

"I'd like to know. Please tell me, Liam."

"I'd rather show you," he said. She stood quite still as his fingers traced a delicate line from her eyes along her cheeks, stopping at the pulse beating in her throat. When his hands cupped her face, she looked up at him trustingly, and with a groan he pulled her to him, molding her body to his and gently cradling her head against his chest.

"Amie," he said, and she could feel his breath stirring her hair. "I want to make love to you. Will you come back to the hotel with me?"

"Yes."

For a second his eyes blazed with desire, and she waited longingly for the touch of his lips against hers. But he didn't kiss her. He drew in a sharp breath, and his mouth twisted into a tight smile. "Please move away from me," he said, "or we may never make it out of the parking lot."

She took a shaky step backward. The outside of her body felt cold as soon as she stepped away from him, but inside she was burning with an uncontrollable fever.

"We can't leave right away," he said. "I have to pay

the check, or else the restaurant owners will be sending out search parties for us."

"I'd forgotten about the bill." She looked away as she spoke, wrapping her arms around her body. The urge to reach out and caress the taut line of his jaw was almost overpowering.

"Let me take you back to the car," Liam said. They walked across the deserted lot, their hands not quite touching. "My money and credit cards are in my jacket pocket," he said as he unlocked the car door. "Will you be warm enough if I take back my jacket?"

She wanted to say that she didn't think she would ever be warm again away from the protection of his embrace, but she bit her lips and managed to keep silent. She handed the coat to him, then leaned against the side of the car. She wasn't at all sure she could stand upright without support.

When he had put on the jacket, he turned to look at her. It seemed to be almost against his better judgment that he bent down and kissed her again, a probing, tender kiss that left her shaking with longing.

The space between them seemed filled with tension as Liam started to walk away. "Thank God it's only twelve miles to the hotel," he said.

CHAPTER SEVEN

THEY SCARCELY SPOKE during the short drive home. Liam's expression was remote, thoughtful, and Amie hoped intensely that he wasn't thinking of his wife. For herself, she wanted only to feel, not to think, and she blanked out her mind with an almost desperate determination.

Liam parked the car and took their room keys from the elderly man at the reception desk. As they climbed the shallow wooden stairs to the first floor, Amie was acutely aware of the old-fashioned smell of lavender polish and the muted sounds of their footsteps on the woven wool carpet. She didn't want to think about what she was doing. It seemed as if in compensation her senses had sprung into intense, vibrant life.

When they reached Liam's room, he gave her no

opportunity to change her mind about joining him. He pulled her inside, locking the door behind them. He didn't even turn on the light before he took her in his arms, lifting her easily and carrying her to the bed. He kissed her fiercely, hungrily, his caressing hands setting her body ablaze even through the barrier of her clothes. His mouth was hard on her lips. The weight of his body flattened her breasts against his chest, and she felt the urgent thrust of his body against her thighs. His hand traced the curve of her breast and the sexual tension that had been building within her all evening spiraled out of control. She stroked her fingertips down the sides of his face, feeling a faint roughness where his beard had started to grow. "Love me, Liam," she murmured. "Please love me."

He kissed her again, lingeringly, then rolled away and leaned across the bed to switch on the lamp. She sat up immediately, disoriented by the sudden light. Instinctively she straightened the rumpled skirt of her dress and reached up to touch her hair, smoothing it in an agitated gesture. She wished Liam hadn't banished the comforting shield of darkness. It was so much easier to keep her thoughts under control when it was dark.

His hand closed over hers, stilling their nervous movement. "Let me take down your hair," he said huskily. "I've been wanting to do that all week, ever since that night when I came back from Florida."

She bent her head in silent agreement and he reached out, removing the pins from her hair one by one. They dropped unheeded onto the bed. He watched intently, his eyes darkening with desire, as her hair gradually swirled into a silken cloud around her shoulders. When all the pins were gone, he twisted his hands into the long strands and, pulled her head against his chest, burying his face in the heavy golden mass.

"I wanted to look at you," he said. "That's why I switched on the light."

"You see me almost every day."

He smiled. "No, I don't see *you*. I see Ms. Fletcher." He kissed the base of her throat, letting her hair drift over his face, his hands caressing her skillfully until it seemed that every part of her body tingled in response to his touch.

"Liam . . ." she murmured, not looking at him. "Liam, I want you so much."

He took her face in his hands, forcing her to look directly at him. "Say that again," he ordered.

"I want you," she whispered.

His groan of pleasure was muffled against her skin as he gathered her into a deep, passionate embrace. His trail of kisses ended abruptly at the low neckline of her dress. "Do you realize that you're wearing far too many clothes?" he said. "You're definitely overdressed for the occasion."

Passion thickened his voice, and her body responded with an immediate shiver of desire. "So are you," she said huskily.

He stood up at once and flung off his jacket, tugging at the knot of his tie. Swiftly he unbuttoned his shirt and tossed it to the floor. She watched him in a hypnotized silence as his hands paused at the buckle of his belt, a small smile hovering at the corners of his mouth. "Are you enjoying the striptease?" he asked. "I hope I'm going to get a similar show in exchange."

His words sent liquid fire coursing through her body. "I can't reach the zipper on my dress."

"A problem that's easily taken care of." He sat beside

her on the bed and looked steadily into her eyes as he lowered the zipper. "How do you like my room-service special?" he asked softly.

"It seems . . . it seems very efficient. I'll recommend it to the management."

Laughter warmed his eyes. Still looking at her searchingly, he slipped the slender black straps from her shoulders and slid the dress down to her waist. He laid her back against the pillows, and she felt cool air ripple over her skin. Then her body flushed with heat as his mouth descended slowly to her breasts. Waves of pleasure expanded from her scalp and stretched down to her toes as he caressed her nipples with his tongue, tormenting her with longing. Nothing in her relationship with Jeff had prepared her for the sensations now racking her body, and she felt a moment of fear because her physical response to Liam was so immediate and intense. Her fingers moved restlessly through the springy thickness of his hair when he pushed the dress down over her hips, and she reached for him blindly, aching for his kiss.

He caressed her face lightly, and she turned her mouth to press a kiss into his palm. His hand shook beneath her lips. "Amie . . ." he murmured, his mouth against her breasts. "Your skin feels so soft." He looked up at her, smiling tenderly, although his eyes glittered with the sheen of desire. "You smell of peaches."

"It's talcum powder." She found it difficult to speak clearly. Her body seemed too weak to perform even the simplest physical task, yet at the same time she felt more acutely alive than she ever had before. She felt no more doubts about the rightness of what she was doing. She knew only that she ached to feel his naked body next to hers, covering her and making her complete.

She reached up and put her hands on either side of Liam's face, pulling his mouth down onto her own in a long, fierce kiss. She grasped the tanned skin of his back, reveling in the feel of firm, muscled flesh beneath her fingertips. When he kissed the shadowed valley between her breasts, she raked her nails lightly across his shoulders in an immediate, involuntary reaction.

His breath emerged in a harsh gasp, whether of pain or pleasure she couldn't guess. With swift, sure movements he removed the remainder of her clothes, his mouth trailing hot kisses in the wake of his hands. She had never experienced anything like the strange pulsating fire that raced through her body when they finally lay naked together on the bed. She thought Liam must be feeling the same agonizing pleasure. There was a throbbing undercurrent of urgency in the tender passion of his touch, and the fire inside her grew hotter and hotter. She was burning, consumed with the need for his possession.

He pushed her deep against the pillows, and the uneven rasp of his breathing sounded in her ear. She clung to him, her mouth open on his shoulder, as he finally joined his body with hers. The thrust of him against her thighs was the most exquisite pleasure she had ever known. The agonizing tension inside her coiled tighter and tighter until it finally flared into an explosion of warmth and joy. Her cry of fulfillment, half rapture, half torment, was crushed against Liam's mouth. She felt the same wild explosion erupt in his body, and she clung to him as her heartbeat slowed and the strange warmth seeped slowly out of her pores.

He held her for a long time, not saying anything, simply lying still and quiet beside her. Then he reached up and pushed the sweat-dampened hair out of her eyes.

"Amie," he said softly. "What are you thinking about?"

I love you, she thought. I'm thinking how much I love you. A chill of cold air swept over Amie's skin, piercing her euphoria and cooling the fevered excitement of her body. She sat up in bed and felt fear creeping along her veins, the same veins that only a few minutes earlier had burned with passion. She was overwhelmed with panic at the realization of what she had just done. She had made love with a man who would despise her utterly if he ever remembered the truth about her past. She had been crazy enough to fall in love with the man who had tried to send her to jail! She huddled at the edge of the bed.

"Amie, what is it? What's the matter, for God's sake?"

With a tremendous effort she forced her vocal chords to function. "Nothing's the matter," she said. "I was just thinking you give a great performance in bed." She was astonished at the way her voice sounded. Inside she felt only pain, but for some reason her voice emerged sounding cool and faintly ironic.

All trace of gentleness disappeared from Liam's expression, and for a moment Amie could clearly see the implacable man who had confronted her in the Riverside courtroom. "What does that remark mean?" he demanded.

She wrapped one of the covers tightly around her, bending down so that her hair fell forward, hiding her face. "It means you're a great lover, Liam. If you ever need a recommendation, you can count on me."

He got up from the bed and walked over to the window, tugging on the old-fashioned blind to open it. The snap of the roller shattered the last remnant of their intimacy.

"I guess there's not much point in continuing this conversation," he said. "But believe it or not, I didn't take you to bed to prove I'm a superstar between the sheets."

"Didn't you? So why did you do it, Liam?"

He stared out of the window for a few moments before answering her. "I think anything I say in answer to that question is likely to incriminate me as far as you're concerned," he said flatly. "But don't you think you should examine your own actions a bit before you question mine?"

"I don't know what you mean."

"Don't you? I've never lied to you, Amie, about anything. Can you say the same thing to me?"

She was sick with fright. "Why should I lie to you?" she asked, wondering if he heard the panic she could no longer keep out of her voice. "Anyway, I don't want to talk about it . . . about what happened. I'm going to my room. There's nothing to discuss." She grabbed her discarded clothes, fumbling ineffectually as she struggled to zip up her dress.

Liam bent down and retrieved one of her sandals from beneath a chair. "Here," he said. "You'll need this."

"Thank you." She turned blindly toward the door, feeling all thumbs as she attempted to turn the key in the lock. The knowledge that she had fallen in love with Liam Kane kept pounding at the edge of her consciousness, demanding to be let in. Her breath froze in her lungs when Liam came up behind her.

"I'll unlock the door," he said coldly. He waited until she was out in the corridor, then looked straight at her, forcing her to meet his gaze. "The board meeting is at nine o'clock tomorrow morning. I'll meet you downstairs at seven forty-five. Make sure you're on time."

"Yes." It was impossible to say anything more. She crossed the corridor, unlocked the door to her room, and slammed it shut behind her.

She undressed and got into bed, although she knew sleep would be impossible. Her body still ached with the need for Liam's touch, and her heart thudded with the accelerated rhythm only he could cure. She stared into the darkness and the knowledge of her love flooded over her. She loved the sharpness of Liam's intellect and the integrity of his character. She loved talking with him, and she loved his flashes of teasing humor. Her spirit craved his company, and her body thirsted for the ultimate consummation of his lovemaking.

Hysterical laughter welled in her throat, and she turned her face into the pillow, smothering the wrenching gasps. What a terrible moment she had chosen to discover the fatal flaw in her scheme for revenge! How perfectly her seduction of Liam Kane had worked except for one small detail! How could she have guessed that she would fall in love with him?

As soon as she posed the question, the answer came to her. She could easily have known the truth about her feelings if she had ever allowed herself to examine them. She had needed to work hard at ignoring the truth, she thought bitterly. Refusing to face up to facts was one skill she had honed to the level of a fine art over the past four years.

Amie tossed fitfully in the antique bed. She might as well have been resting on a straw pallet for all the ease she could find. The covers twisted in an uncomfortable heap around her thighs. She sighed wearily. It promised to be a long night.

* * *

Liam was already waiting for her when she arrived downstairs the next morning, five minutes before the agreed upon time. She refused his curt offer of breakfast, and the drive into Stamford passed in total silence.

They walked into the boardroom side by side, the perfect picture of a dynamic executive and his efficient secretary. Amie smiled courteously at the directors and took copious notes, but she was scarcely aware of her surroundings. It was a shock when she heard a ripple of applause greet the end of Liam's presentation. The directors, she realized, were impressed with the brilliance of his strategic planning. She felt a small, irrational spurt of pride at his achievement and was glad that something about this disastrous weekend had turned out well.

They ate lunch with the chairman of the board in his private suite, and it was late afternoon before they started the drive back to New York's La Guardia airport. Amie stared out of the car window and tried to clarify her impressions of the meetings they had just attended. If she didn't straighten out her thoughts soon, she knew her lengthy notes would prove useless.

She felt Liam scrutinizing her averted features, but pretended not to notice. "The New York style of driving doesn't seem to be bothering you anymore," he said unexpectedly, breaking the strained silence. "That's a rapid adjustment."

For the first time she really paid attention to the chaotic scene on the highway outside their car. The wail of a police siren announced its rapid approach behind them, and a speeding truck slowed and pulled over to the side of the road. Just then a delivery van roared past, avoiding the side panels of their Buick by less than an inch. She bit back a gasp of nervous laughter. How could she say that her awareness of his presence was too overwhelming to leave room for trivial worries about speeding delivery trucks? "No," she said finally. "I guess the traffic doesn't bother me anymore. I suppose I must be good at adjusting to new situations."

She could feel his eyes flick over her once again, and she stared down at her hands. "I have some papers to work on," he said, after only the briefest of pauses. "If the plane has a spare seat, I'd like to spread them out since the flow charts look pretty complex. You won't mind if we don't sit together?"

"No, of course not. I'll take the opportunity to write up my notes from this morning's meeting."

"Good old Ms. Fletcher, she never lets up, does she? I can always rely on her to give me an answer straight out of the *Good Secretaries' Handbook*."

Amie clenched her hands more tightly together. "Ms. Fletcher is a darned efficient secretary," she said.

Liam's short bark of laughter contained no amusement. "Then I'd better be nice to her, I guess. God knows, good secretaries are almost impossible to find. I hope nothing that's happened this weekend will affect my excellent working relationship with the super-efficient Ms. Fletcher."

Pain began to radiate along Amie's flesh and she quickly closed her eyes, shutting out her view of his taunting profile. If only she could tell him the truth about the past. If only so many deceptions didn't lie between them. Lord, how she hated it when he called her "Ms. Fletcher!" "The car rental return is to your right," she said, her voice sounding harsh with the effort to suppress her feelings.

Liam swore fluently under his breath, then swung the Buick around sharply, waiting with evident impatience for the electronic gate to open. "Drop the rental agreement in the slot, will you?" he ordered. "Let's see if we can make the early flight. There's no reason to hang around here."

The next morning Amie arrived at her desk precisely at nine, expecting to find Liam already at work. Perversely, today of all days, he was nowhere to be seen. There was no sign of him in his office and no message from him on her desk. She roamed restlessly through the rooms, rehearsing her resignation over and over again. She had to get the cool, faintly regretful intonation just right or Liam might start asking some awkward questions. She, more than most people, knew that he wasn't an easy man to deceive.

Her rehearsals were unnecessary. At nine-thirty she received a telephone message from Liam's answering service saying he would not be in the office that day. "He asked you to take care of canceling his meetings, dear. He didn't have time," the answering-service operator told her.

"But didn't he say where he was going? Didn't he leave some number where I can reach him?"

"No, dear." The operator sounded middle-aged and placid. "Mr. Kane just gave us the message I passed on to you already."

"Did he . . . did he sound sick or ill or anything?"

"No." The operator's patience had begun to wear a little thin. "He just said he had been called unexpectedly out of town."

"Well, thank you for letting me know."

"My pleasure, dear."

Liam's absence meant that Amie was kept too busy

to brood about her personal affairs. By five o'clock she felt she had answered at least a thousand telephone calls, and she sighed when the phone console on her desk buzzed yet again. She picked up the receiver and reached wearily for her message pad.

"Mr. Kane's office," she said. "This is Amie Fletcher."

"Well *hello*, sugar baby. I'd have recognized your voice anywhere. How are you doing?"

She held the phone a couple of inches away and made a face at it. "I'm doing very well, thank you," she said crisply, not bothering to hide her impatience. She wasn't in the mood for flirtatious conversations with junior project managers at this hour of the afternoon. "Who is this speaking, please?"

"I'm hurt, honey. How could you forget me after all those Sunday evening phone calls we used to make to one another?"

Her fingers tightened around the receiver and her stomach muscles clenched in revulsion. "Jeff?" she whispered. "Jeff Cooper, is that you?"

"That's it," he said cheerfully. "You guessed it in one, Amie my sweet. So tell me what you've been doing these past four years. I heard from a friend that you made it to the big time. He told me you're personal assistant to the big chief of the National Development Corporation."

"Yes, I am. Well...er...how are you, Jeff? When did you get out...I mean, when did you arrive in Chicago?"

"Oh, I came here as soon as I got out of jail," he said. "I wanted to be somewhere where I had some friends, and your parents told me you were in the Windy City."

"Oh. Well...er...how are you doing?" she asked again. "Is everything okay?"

"Everything will be fine real soon, if I can get some help from my friends. I'm counting on you to stand by me, seeing as how you got off so damn lightly from your little problems down in Riverside. After all, I'm the one who got left holding the bag."

"Those problems at West Farm weren't my fault," she said tautly. "You know that better than anybody."

He laughed. "Well now, sweetie, there's no need to sound so defensive about things. The best of us can make a mistake now and again, just like I told your father when I spoke to him last week."

She closed her eyes. "What do you want from me, Jeff?"

"I told you. I thought you might be interested in helping me out—for old time's sake, you know."

"Do you need money?" she asked tightly.

"Sure do." His voice hardened. "You don't acquire much capital hammering out car license plates for four years."

"I could lend you some money, to help you get started again."

"Well now, Amie my sweet, I guess I have a whole lot of expensive tastes that have been building up real bad while I was . . . away. I don't suppose you have enough money in your bank account to keep me happy for more than a week or two. But I'd like to meet you tonight and talk over some plans I've made for the future."

She felt a shiver of anxiety ripple down her spine. "I'm sorry, Jeff, but I don't think there would be any point in our meeting. I'm not interested in planning for the future. Not right now."

"Well now, baby, I suggest you don't make any real hasty decisions. I think we have lots to talk about. Old times, old friends . . ."

"I'm rather busy at the moment, Jeff."

"That's too bad, you know, Amie, because I hate to think what your fancy new employer would do if I told him what happened in the last place you worked. The way I hear it, bosses usually get uncomfortable around employees who've mislaid thousands of dollars in their previous job."

"I didn't mislay thousands of dollars. You're twisting the truth, you know you are."

"I think you and I have things to talk about, baby, like I said. I suggest you meet me tonight."

Just then, to Amie's horror, Liam walked into the office and halted by her desk. "Good evening," he said softly. "Do you need me to take that call?"

She shook her head, panic-stricken in case he had heard Jeff's voice. "I can't talk anymore," she said into the phone. "My boss just arrived back."

"That's all right, baby, I don't want to keep you from your work. But I'll expect to see you this evening for a drink at the Black Keg. That's only a block from your office. Do you think you'll be off work by six?"

"I don't know." She heard Liam behind her, searching through the pile of papers she had put on his desk. "All right," she told Jeff, desperate to cut him off before he forced her to say something incriminating. "I'll try to meet you at six, but I may be a couple of minutes late."

"I'll wait," he said, and the tone of his voice made her hands feel suddenly cold on the receiver.

"Good-bye," she said, and hung up the phone as quickly as she could. She hurried into Liam's office, pasting a bright smile onto her face. "I didn't expect you back tonight," she said. "Did you get through your business earlier than you expected?"

He looked at her consideringly, without a trace of a

smile. "Yes," he said. He forced her to continue looking at him, and a wave of desire swept over her, adding warmth to her cool cheeks. "Have dinner with me tonight, Amie. We have things to talk about. A lot of things."

"I can't," she said, tearing her eyes away from his. "Really I can't, Liam. I have to go somewhere tonight."

"I didn't realize you would be busy all evening," he said, and she couldn't interpret the curiously restrained intonation of his voice. "Then perhaps we can have dinner some other time." His manner suggested that it was of little importance to him one way or the other. He indicated the stack of papers on his desk. "Any special problems today?"

"Nothing extraordinary, although it's been busy. As you can see, there's a pile of messages for you. All urgent, of course."

"I'll take care of them. You'd better clear off your desk or you'll be late. I heard you make arrangements to meet somebody at six o'clock."

She wondered how much else he had heard. "Liam," she began desperately, "I don't think I can go on work—"

"I'm sorry, Amie, but I don't have time to discuss anything with you right now. I have to deal with all these urgent messages, and I have a report to write up. I'll see you tomorrow."

She turned away, not knowing whether to feel relief or regret over the reprieve he was insisting on giving her. She supposed it wasn't essential to hand in her resignation right this minute. "All right," she said. "Until tomorrow then. Good night, Liam."

CHAPTER EIGHT

AMIE SAW JEFF sitting in a small corner booth as soon as she entered the Black Keg. She recognized him immediately, although she had forgotten until this moment how incredibly handsome he was. His hair gleamed with bright golden highlights, and in the dim light of the bar his skin looked tanned and his eyes shone with an attractive blue brilliance. He looked up and caught her glance, smiling with practiced charm. For a moment there was no recognition in his gaze; then his smile broadened as he realized who she was.

He stood up to greet her when she stopped at his table, an unmistakable gleam of admiration in his eyes. "This *is* Amie Fletcher, I presume?" His smile was wider than ever, and he shook her hand with enthusiasm, pulling her against him to administer a quick, expert kiss. His hand slipped smoothly around her shoulders. "Well *hello* again, honey," he said. "I didn't recognize you at first, you've changed so much. You're looking spectacular, baby, simply spectacular. I had no idea you could look so great."

"Thank you," she said dryly, but her subtle sarcasm was apparently lost on him. Calmly, she disengaged herself from his grasp. "You look pretty good yourself, Jeff."

"Yes," he said, and a note of bitterness entered his voice. "Considering where I've been for the last four years I feel pretty good, too."

"When did you . . . er . . . get out?"

"A couple of weeks ago. Long enough to call up a few of my old friends. And long enough to go south and soak up some sun."

"I can see you have a tan," she said, then fell silent, unable to think of anything else to say. They were simply two strangers, two strangers who knew too much about each other's past. She felt a quiver of revulsion when she saw the emptiness of his smile, and she turned away, not wanting to look at him any longer. "Why don't we sit down?" she suggested.

He nodded his agreement and sat close beside her on the stuffed velour banquette. "Well, this is just like old times," he said, putting his hand on her knee. "What will you drink, honey? You have a couple to make up if you're hoping to keep pace with me."

"I'll have a glass of white wine," she said. "But let's make it my treat, Jeff. What can I get you?"

"A double bourbon on the rocks," he said, swallowing the dregs of the drink already in front of him. He smiled at her again, his gaze at once confident and predatory.

"I've got a lot of celebrating to catch up on, Amie, and I'll be real glad to have you around while I do it. I can see you've developed a classy sense of style since you came to Chicago. You're the sort of woman any man likes to take out on a date. I always knew you'd turn out to be a real doll once you grew up and moved away from those dreary preacher-parents of yours."

"I think you're right," she said. "I have grown up. At last."

"And I sure do like the adult model you've grown into! But you were always a cute kid, you know, Amie, and we had some good times together back in Riverside. Even then I thought you'd probably turn out okay." He patted her knee with infuriating self-confidence. "And you'd better believe I was right in my predictions! You're really something, baby."

"So are you, Jeff."

He smiled, taking her words at face value. "Now that you're not so damned naïve, I guess we could have ourselves some real fun together. Chicago's not such a bad town in the summer. I'll bet we could find one or two places where we could have a spectacular night out. Maybe you already know somewhere good on Rush Street. Those nightclubs along there change hands so fast, I don't know what's hot anymore."

Amie closed her eyes, then opened them again to stare fixedly into her drink. *This* was the man she had imagined herself in love with! How could she ever have been so lacking in judgment as to enjoy his company? Or had four years in jail totally changed him? "There doesn't seem to be a waitress around," she said when she finally had command of her voice. She stood up, glad to be released from the feel of his hand against her knee. "I'm thirsty, Jeff. I think I'll order our drinks directly from the bartender."

She hurried across the darkened room, delighted to get away from him even if only for a few minutes. She wondered again how she had ever managed to persuade herself that she was in love with him. Only a very young and innocent girl could have been deceived by Jeff Cooper's handsome face and insincere smiles.

The bartender served her all too quickly. She carried the drinks back to their table, determined to bring her meeting with Jeff to a rapid close. She sat down at a safe distance from his wandering hands and took a small sip of wine. "How can I help you, Jeff?" she said. "I could lend you some money if you need a loan to tide you over the next couple of months."

"I told you, Amie, I need more money than you could give me. But thanks all the same."

"Then how can I help?"

"I want a job with National Development. The economy's lousy and the job market's worse. But I hear Mr. Kane would hire the devil himself if you told him to."

She flushed. "That's not so, Jeff."

"Isn't it? That's not what I heard. Well, anyway, will you put in a good word for me? I need an inside recommendation. It's hard to explain away four years without references."

She could never recommend him to Liam, of course, even if she wanted to. Liam had apparently forgotten about her part in the West Farm fraud case, but he would surely recognize Jeff Cooper's name the minute he heard it. How ironic that Jeff should be asking her to help in the one way most likely to cause him trouble. If only he knew who Liam Kane really was!

"Jeff, I can't ask Mr. Kane for any special favors. I'm sorry, but I really can't. Would you like me to talk to Mr. Hubert, the personnel manager? What sort of job are you looking for?"

"I'm an accountant," he said. "Naturally I'd like to work in the accounts department of National Development."

She swallowed hard, coloring with embarrassment, then looked down at her hands. "I . . . I couldn't recommend you for a job as an accountant. Please don't ask me."

His expression immediately lost all trace of friendliness and his blue eyes glittered with sudden cruelty. "Why not?" he asked. "Don't you think four years in the state's worst prison was long enough to reform my morals?"

"I don't know . . ."

"Say that again," he said. "I didn't hear you."

She was frightened by the violence she sensed in him, a violence that was looking for an excuse to be unleashed. "Jeff, I couldn't recommend you for a position where you dealt with other people's money," she whispered. "You caused such hardship to so many people when you stole those investment funds from West Farm—"

"I didn't steal the money. I borrowed it. I intended to put it back; I just got caught at a time when my investments were down. If the stock market had turned around, and if that smart-aleck Lawrence King hadn't stuck his nose into things that didn't concern him, I'd have been home free."

"I'll talk to the personnel manager tomorrow," she said. "I'll see what jobs he has available. But not in accounts, Jeff. I just couldn't."

His hand whipped out across the table, clutching her wrist in a painfully tight grasp. "I want a job in accounts," he said. "I just want you to recommend me. To the president, to Liam Kane. Not to some jerk of a personnel manager."

"No."

He removed his hand and suddenly his face was all smiles again. "You know, Amie, I hoped we could keep this as a real friendly discussion because I like you, I really do. But I can see you're not going to be reasonable. I want an accounting job at National Development, with access to the company's computer records, and if you don't help me get it, I'm going to have to make an appointment to see your friend Mr. Kane. I think he'd be very interested to find out what his super-charming secretary was up to when she lived in Riverside. I think he'd be very interested in my version of what happened at West Farm Insurance—about how a hotshot graduate of the local college came in and messed up my accounts and left me to carry the ball. And she was my lover and all. That experience surely taught me you never can trust a woman. You never know what she's up to behind your back."

She looked directly at him. "That's blackmail, Jeff."

"Unless you lied to your employers, you have nothing to worry about," he said. "What's so special about Liam Kane that you're afraid to ask him for a small favor? What are you afraid I might tell him that he doesn't already know?"

"Nothing," she said, no longer afraid because she suddenly knew exactly what she had to do. She wasn't going to submit herself or National Development Corporation to Jeff Cooper's criminal schemes. She drank the remainder of her glass of wine, thinking rapidly. "I'm meeting Liam for dinner tomorrow night," she lied. "I'll find an opportunity to talk to him then. Give me a call this weekend, will you? I'll let you know what he says."

He looked at her narrowly. "I know where you live, Amie. You wouldn't try to pull any fancy tricks, would you? I want that job in accounts."

"No tricks," she said. "I have to go now, Jeff, but you can call me over the weekend."

"I'll call Friday night," he said. "That gives you four days to work on your Mr. Liam Kane." She nodded her agreement, and he was all smiles again. "You want me to take you home, Amie, for old times' sake?"

She barely managed to repress a shudder. "Thank you, but I'll take a cab," she said. "A couple of my neighbors said they might stop by this evening. You don't want to find yourself in the middle of a neighborhood coffee party."

"It doesn't sound like my kind of scene," he agreed. "But I'll look forward to having a long talk with you on Friday. Make sure you haven't got any neighbors hanging around then. When you've had a chance to think things over, I'm sure you'll decide that there's no reason why we shouldn't pick things up just where we left off. And this time we'd be real partners. I'm planning on having you work right in there with me."

She had to leave the table before she threw something at him. "I've got to dash, Jeff, or my neighbors will be sending out search parties. But I'll be waiting for your call on Friday." She gathered up her sweater and purse and almost ran out of the bar. She couldn't wait to get home and take a long, hot shower, although she knew she was going to need more than a few gallons of soapy water to wash away the lingering feeling of contamination that Jeff had left imprinted on her skin.

As soon as she had showered, she slipped into a thin cotton robe and dialed Liam's home telephone number. To her relief, he answered the call himself. "Liam," she said quickly, "something's come up, a family emergency. I have to leave Chicago right away."

"Of course," he said, after only a brief pause. "Is there any way I can help? When are you leaving?"

"Tonight. I have to leave right now. And Liam, I don't think I'll be coming back. I'm resigning from the National Development Corporation. I'm sorry I haven't given you the proper notice, but it's an emergency."

There was another brief silence on the other end of the phone. "I'd like you to reconsider that decision," he said.

"No, I can't!" Hearing the note of panic in her voice, she forced herself to speak more softly so that she no longer sounded so frantic. She didn't want him to start thinking that her whole family had been wiped out in some disaster. On the other hand, she didn't want to specify the exact nature of the "family emergency." There had already been far too many lies in her dealings with Liam. "I won't be coming back to Chicago for a while," she said, keeping her voice steady by a great effort of will. "You must look for a new secretary, Liam. I heard that Anne Cheatham in the design department is pretty good. They say she's efficient and reliable."

"Are you leaving for Missouri tonight?"

"Missouri?" she asked, momentarily bewildered. Then she remembered that central Missouri was supposed to be her birthplace and she quickly recovered her mistake.

"Yes, I'm taking the bus to St. Louis tonight," she said. "I'm leaving for the bus station as soon as I can pack a couple of suitcases."

"I'll be sorry to lose you," Liam said. "Please remember where you can find me, and let me know if there's ever any way I can be of help. When you come back to Chicago, I'm sure you know there'll always be some sort of job waiting for you at National."

There was something wrong with the direction this conversation was taking. She would never have expected Liam to accept her resignation so . . . so bloodlessly . . . as if he felt mild regret, but nothing more. "Liam," she said huskily, "I wish I didn't have to go."

She clamped her lips together to cut off the rest of the useless words of regret that hovered on the tip of her tongue. She had no right to involve him in her problems. She had already made the decision to leave National Development, and that decision was irrevocable—it had to be. Once she left Chicago, Jeff Cooper would have no chance to put his fraudulent plans into action. Unless she was prepared to trust Liam with the whole sordid truth about her past, it was clearly her duty to get out of National Development and out of Jeff's reach as fast as she could.

"Have you thought of some way I can help?" Liam asked. "Was there some problem you wanted to share with me? You sound a bit uncertain about things."

"No," she said quickly. "Thanks for the offer, but this is a . . . a family matter. I have to deal with it myself."

"Well, if you're sure. You know I'd like to help." He paused, but she said nothing and he spoke quietly into the phone. "Good-bye, Amie. Take care."

As she hung up the phone, Amie became aware of

the wetness on her cheeks. She wiped the tears away, angry with herself for wishing she could stay in Chicago. Even before Jeff's telephone call she'd known there was no future in her relationship with Liam. She'd been planning to resign anyway. Jeff's threatened blackmail had merely pushed her to act immediately. The sooner she left the city, she told herself, the better it would be for everybody. The bracing words were sound advice, but they did nothing to ease the heavy ache of longing that clamped like a vise around her heart.

She packed methodically, forcing herself to concentrate on the practical tasks at hand. She would move into a suburban motel for a couple of days while she made all the arrangements for closing her apartment. After that, she wasn't at all sure where she would go. Fortunately, she had enough money in her bank account to keep her for a month or so if she lived frugally. Suddenly the ring of the doorbell interrupted her thoughts, and her hands tightened around the blouse she was holding. Jeff Cooper, she thought. Oh, Lord, he hasn't waited until Friday!

She was afraid to answer the door, but the bell continued to ring. She crept into the hall, wondering if he would ever go away, wondering if he had seen the crack of light beneath her front door. What would he do if he forced his way into her bedroom and saw the suitcases spread out over the bed? He would be furiously angry once he realized that she was sneaking away, taking with her his chance of employment in the accounts department at National Development. After four years in the state prison, he probably wouldn't hesitate to use physical violence.

The ringing of the doorbell stopped, and for a moment there was absolute silence in the apartment hallway, a silence that seemed more unnerving than the constant ring of the bell. The blood pounded in her ears and her pulse raced before the momentary calm was shattered.

"Amie, I know you're in there! Open this damn door, or I swear to God I'll kick it down!"

"Liam?"

"Of course it's Liam. Who the hell did you expect it to be? Your *family emergency* miraculously revived?"

She opened the door and he stormed into the small lobby, angrier than she had ever seen him. No wonder he had sounded unnaturally calm on the phone. He simply hadn't wanted to scare her into running away before he could drive to Evanston. "What's this stupid story all about?" he demanded, slamming the door behind him. "Did you really expect me to fall for such a transparent lie? If so, I'm not flattered by your opinion of my intelligence. And if you're leaving because of what happened over the weekend, then tell me so. Don't lie about it. There's no need for lies between us, not ever. Can't you learn to trust me, Amie? Damn it, can't you see that you have to trust me if we're ever going to have any sort of a relationship?"

She thought of at least a dozen different replies, all hopelessly inadequate. She looked at him, longing for the courage to tell him everything, so that they could wipe away all the squalid deceptions of the past. His eyes held hers, refusing to let her turn away, and suddenly—humiliatingly—she burst into tears.

For a moment Liam stared at her across the few feet of space that still separated them. Then all the anger drained from his body, and a wry smile crooked his mouth. He gathered her into his arms, stroking her back and smoothing the hair gently away from her damp face.

"Don't cry," he murmured. "It's not fair when women cry. Don't you know that men can resist everything except that?"

Amie nestled her cheek against his soft cotton shirt, and the sobs racking her body slowly subsided. Her tears soaked into his shirt, and it seemed as though they took with them all the hurt and degradation of her encounter with Jeff Cooper. She thought she would be happy to stand close to Liam forever, feeling the hard line of his jaw resting against the top of her head. She stirred against him, utterly content. She couldn't remember a time since she was a small child when she had felt so secure, so protected.

It was Liam who spoke first. "It's not that I object to lending you my shoulder," he said, "but are you ready now to tell me what's troubling you? And Amie, please, no more lies about family emergencies."

She turned away from him, the warm sense of security vanishing as she did so. "It wasn't exactly a lie. Something has come up, Liam, and I have to leave Chicago right away. Please don't question me about it."

"Is your mother sick? Your father? Has somebody in your family had an accident?"

She didn't want to add yet another untruth to the mountain of falsehoods that already separated them, but she could see he wasn't going to be satisfied with vague generalizations. "It's my father," she said. "He's had a heart attack. He's very sick. I have to go to him right away. If you stay here, I'll miss the bus."

He looked at her in silence, his mouth drawn into a hard line. "When you lie to me your eyes darken and your cheeks flush right in the middle in two small circles," he said. "When the lie makes you particularly uncomfortable, you hold your hands together, with the fingers tightly interlaced. You also start to speak more rapidly, and your sentences become short and somewhat jerky. Now will you tell me the truth about why you're running away? Hasn't it occurred to you that whatever the problem is, maybe I can help?"

She glanced down at her hands and saw the betraying gleam of tense white knuckles. Her fingers were clenched so tightly that they were already numb.

"Full marks for detection," she said as she pulled herself out of his arms. "Are you freshening up your detective skills, hoping to get back your old job in the Commerce Department? Is the business world proving tame after so many years chasing criminals?" Her voice was starting to quaver, and she hurried toward her bedroom. "I've got nothing more to say to you," she said. "I'm leaving Chicago, Liam, and I'd appreciate it if you would go home to your own apartment. I have a great deal to do tonight."

She expected him to be angry. She had, in fact, half hoped to provoke him to anger so that he would go away while she still had the strength to stick to her intention of leaving the city. But he defeated her plans by saying softly, "I can't leave until you've said good-bye."

She halted in the doorway leading to her bedroom, taking care not to turn and look at him. "G–good-bye, Liam."

"That's not quite what I meant," he said. "You have to kiss your friends when you say good-bye. Didn't anybody ever tell you that?" He came up behind her, and his hand skimmed lightly over her long hair. He pulled her back against his body, circling one arm around her waist and trailing his other hand down her throat. His lean fingers scarcely hesitated when they reached the low, loose neckline of her robe. His touch seared her skin like fire, and she knew he must feel the immediate hardening of her nipples, just as she was aware of his increasing response to her body. If she pulled out of his arms and walked into her bedroom, she guessed that Liam would make no move to stop her, but she had no desire to leave him. She wanted to feel his hands caressing her. In fact, she wanted much more than the mere touch of his hands on her breasts: she wanted him to make love to her. She sighed, relaxing against him as he kissed the nape of her neck.

"We are friends, aren't we, Amie?" he asked huskily, and she nodded, not daring to turn around and look at him.

"You still haven't kissed me," he said. "I just need one good-bye kiss, Amie, and then I'll leave."

Shivering with longing, she turned silently within his arms, abandoning the last remnant of her struggle to hide the truth from herself. She was afraid he would see the love and helpless longing in her eyes, so she lowered her lashes as his mouth slowly descended to her own. His lips brushed hers in a gossamer-light caress; then his mouth hardened and he kissed her with fierce hunger, his tongue thrusting against hers the moment she parted her lips.

"I lied," he said shakily when the kiss was finally over. His words were no more that a teasing whisper against her mouth. "One kiss isn't anywhere near enough to satisfy me. I want to make love to you, Amie. I want to continue what we started last weekend. I want to feel you trembling with need, the way you did on Sunday. I want to feel your body moving with mine, making me complete. Let me make love to you, Amie."

"Yes," she said urgently, no longer capable of worrying about what had happened in the past or what the future might bring. "Please, Liam, make love to me now."

He took her into his arms, and her kisses were hungry with passions held too long in check. When at last they broke apart, his breathing was rapid and his face was flushed dark with desire. She stepped into her bedroom and he followed, not bothering to switch on the light.

"My luggage," she murmured. "I left it on the bed."

Liam snapped the cases shut and pushed them onto the floor. He turned back to her at once and slowly unfastened the knot of her belt, his eyes fixed on her face. He eased the robe off her shoulders until it fell in a heap at her feet and her body was outlined by the glow of light coming from the hallway.

She heard the sharp intake of his breath, and then his arms were around her, pulling her to him so fiercely that his belt buckle scraped against her bare stomach. She smothered the involuntary cry of pain, but he must have heard it anyway, for he laid her gently on the bed and his hands traced the scratch with feather-light sensitivity. The touch of his hands set her ablaze with longing, and she arched instinctively toward him, wanting to eliminate every vestige of space between them.

He kissed her again and she turned to him blindly, reaching inside his shirt to run her hands across his smooth, strong shoulders. He sat up for a moment while he ripped off his shirt, and she stroked him again, feeling his quiver of reaction everywhere she touched. She felt the rapid beat of his heart thudding beneath her fingertips, and she bent her head and began to kiss him. When her hands moved down to find his belt, he drew in his breath on a shuddering gasp, but he said nothing as she unfastened the buckle and reached for the zipper of his slacks, pushing it slowly down.

When he was naked, he gathered her tightly against his body, cradling her in his arms as he covered her mouth in a long, sweet kiss.

"Oh God, Amie," he said when they finally drew apart. "Am I going too fast for you? I need you so badly that I'm almost afraid to touch you."

His words sent a wave of heat coursing through her body. "I guess I feel the same way, Liam. I want you, too. Please don't wait any longer."

She closed her eyes as she felt the heavy, pleasurable weight of his body cover hers. She could hear the uneven rasp of his breathing mingling in unison with her own as their hunger for each other continued to increase. His kisses became more demanding, and when she opened her eyes again she saw her own urgent desires reflected in Liam's heavy-lidded gaze.

He parted her legs with his own, kissing her mouth and breasts as he took her into the ultimate embrace. "You're so beautiful, Amie," he whispered, and his words carried her to the final pinnacle of joy. The convulsive trembling of her body had scarcely begun before Liam, too, reached his climax.

Afterward, he held her in his arms, stroking her and murmuring little words of endearment. He pushed her long hair away from her brow, kissing her tenderly when she nuzzled her face against his chest. She didn't speak, for fear that something she said would shatter the perfect intimacy of the moment. If only . . . if only she could tell him the truth.

Some small movement of her body must have communicated her sudden tension to him. He moved slightly and propped himself up on one elbow, looking down at her. In the muted glow of light from the hall, Amie thought that he looked more perfectly at peace than she had ever seen him. She reached out and touched his cheek very lightly. "Thank you, Liam," she said softly. "I hope...I hope it was good for you, too."

"No," he said, smiling. "It wasn't good. It was unbelievable. Fantastic. In fact, I think we'd better do it all over again so that I can convince myself it really happened."

Amie returned his smile, relief making her light-headed with happiness. "How did we start this whole scene?" she murmured. She leaned against him, pressing a kiss to his heart. "Was it like this...?"

His voice deepened. "I don't remember. Keep right on kissing me, though, and I'll do my best to recall exactly what I'm supposed to do next."

"It's a deal."

She awoke to find Liam lying close beside her, his arm resting possessively across her breasts. She stretched sensuously, liking the way the wiry hairs on his arm tickled her skin when she yawned. Her movements woke him, and he turned to look at her, smiling. "Hi," he said.

"Hi yourself." Her gaze slid past him to the glowing dial of the clock radio. "Help!" she said. "Liam, it's nine o'clock! The office!" She started to scramble out of bed and then the memories of her encounter with Jeff Cooper rushed back, and she sat down on the edge of the mattress with a thud. Good grief! What had she done last night? And what on earth was she going to do now?

She had no time to reach a decision, no time even to think clearly, before Liam reached out and pulled her back into bed. "To hell with the office," he said. "In a minute I'm going to call and inform the executive vice-president that I'm taking today and tomorrow off. I'll be back at work on Friday. Until then he can deal with any urgent problems."

"The telephone is on your side of the bed," she said.

Ignoring her words, he began to trace a delicate pattern around the tips of her breasts. "I'll have to let the executive vice-president know that my secretary will also be unavailable," he said. "I'm planning to tell him that I need her with me." He took her face between his hands, kissing her parted lips. "Oh, yes," he whispered. "I most definitely need her with me."

Amie tried to hang onto the lingering remnants of her common sense. "Liam, I can't stay on as your secretary. I told you last night, I have to resign. There are reasons why I must leave Chicago."

For a moment she thought his face seemed shadowed by a faint expression of regret, then the brief frown was gone. "We'll discuss that later," he said. "Right now I'm on vacation and we have a busy schedule ahead of us."

"Oh? What are you planning to do on this vacation?"

"Make love," he said. "What else? After more than five weeks as my secretary, Ms. Fletcher, I wouldn't have thought you needed to ask such elementary questions."

"I'm sorry, sir," she said. "I think my brain's being affected by approaching starvation. Doesn't breakfast figure anywhere in this schedule of yours?"

Liam looked into her laughing eyes and his breathing quickened. "Probably not," he said, wresting the sheet

from her unresisting hands. "I'm not hungry for food."
His mouth covered hers in a passionate kiss, and Amie's
body flamed into awareness. She reached up to embrace
him and once again they were swept away into the star-
pierced darkness of ecstasy.

CHAPTER NINE

IT WAS NEARLY midday before they had both showered and dressed. Amie brewed some coffee and made some toast, humming to herself as she worked. Liam's gaze followed her around the kitchen, and although he didn't say anything, she could feel his warmth reaching out to her, wrapping her in a cocoon of happiness.

They sat together at the kitchen table, eating yogurt and sipping freshly brewed coffee, and she thought that her kitchen never appeared so welcoming, so full of summer sunshine, as it did this morning. If only her stomach weren't knotted with that hard lump of fear about Jeff. If only it were possible to tell Liam the truth. Maybe now, when she felt so close to him . . . Perhaps he would understand . . . perhaps he wouldn't despise her.

"What are you thinking?" he asked quietly. "From

your expression you seem to be having black thoughts for such a beautiful day."

He was right. It was a beautiful day. Too beautiful to spoil with a squalid confession about the past. Surely she could allow herself these two days of perfect happiness before she told him the truth. "I was just wondering how we were going to spend the rest of the day," she hedged. "It's far too nice to stay inside."

"Is it?" he asked quizzically, and for a moment she thought he was going to press her for a more honest reply. She realized that her hands were clenched in two tight balls of tension, and she wrapped them around her coffee mug, forcing herself to look unconcerned. She managed to smother a sigh of relief when Liam said, "Do you have any suggestions about what we might do?"

"I think we should take the tour boat out on Lake Michigan," Amie said. "I bet you've been so busy working since you arrived in Chicago that you haven't seen any of the tourist sights."

"I didn't know there were any," he said with a grin.

"I know you native New Yorkers think the world stops at the New Jersey Turnpike, but the rest of us know that there are about three thousand more miles of interesting country. Chicago is a beautiful city."

Liam grinned again and got up to place his mug in the sink. "I suspect I'm lucky that the coffee pot is already empty," he said, pretending to check the contents of the table. "Luckily I can't see anything else you might throw."

"Don't be too sure. I'm feeling creative this morning."

"Seriously, I think a trip out on the lake sounds like a great idea. And I've never been to the top of the Sears Tower either."

"The tallest free-standing building in the world and

you haven't explored its heights?" she said mockingly. "I can see you have a long way to go before you can claim Chicago as your hometown."

His hand rested for a moment on her cheek. "With you around, I believe it would be easy to start thinking of Chicago as my home."

Their day was everything Amie had hoped for. They took a cab to the pier on Michigan Avenue and climbed aboard the waiting motorboat. An enterprising street vendor was parading up and down the shore selling ice cream, and Liam bought two large cones for them to eat while the boat chugged along the Chicago River out onto Lake Michigan. They shared the boat with a noisy party of third-graders and a sedate group of Japanese tourists, who evidently took their pleasures very seriously—the muted roar of the boat's engine was punctuated by the constant rhythm of their clicking camera shutters.

Once the boat had successfully navigated the complicated river lock system—one of the seven engineering marvels of the modern world, the tour guide announced proudly—Amie and Liam left their seats and wandered to the rear of the boat. They stood at the railing, his arm resting comfortably around her shoulders, as the spray blew up into their faces and the hot sun beat down, chasing away the chill of the lake breeze. The breathtaking elegance of the lakefront architecture stretched out to one side of them. On the other side there was nothing to see but water flowing endlessly into the distance, seemingly as vast as the ocean.

"I guess you haven't seen the real Chicago until you come out on the water like this," Liam remarked. "Of course I knew Chicago was the birthplace of the Amer-

ican skyscraper and the home of a lot of famous architects, but I never realized what incredibly beautiful work
those architects had done in their own city."

"I'm glad you like it," Amie said. "I haven't traveled
enough to make comparisons, but this view always seems
spectacular to me."

The visit to the observation deck of the Sears Tower
was equally successful. Liam kept her hand clasped within
his own as they strolled from one huge window to the
next. Amie felt that time had rolled back so she was once
again the carefree young woman who thought the world
was an exciting place just waiting to be explored. She
was light-headed with fatigue and happiness when Liam
hailed a cab and directed it to his apartment building, a
new tower situated right on the lakefront.

She felt shy as he ushered her into his living room,
and she stood a little awkwardly as he casually tossed
his tourist brochures onto the coffee table.

"I'll fix us something cool to drink," he said, and she
walked over to the window, parting the slats of the vene-
tian blinds so that she could look out over Lake Michigan.
Liam's manner was so relaxed, so intimate, so loving . . . She yearned to take the leap of trust necessary to
confide in him. How wonderful it would be to lie in his
arms, knowing that there was only truth and trust and
honesty between them.

"I mixed you a weak vodka and tonic," Liam said,
coming to stand beside her. "Do you want to eat dinner
out tonight, or would you prefer to stay in?"

She took a sip of the ice-cold drink, pushing her dark
thoughts to one side. "I'd rather stay in, if we could. I'm
not dressed for a night out on the town. Is it difficult for
you to make a meal?"

"No problem. I'll take care of it right away."

"Are you one of the new breed of male gourmet cooks?" she teased. "A whiz in the kitchen who knocks out Cordon Bleu meals at the drop of a carving knife?"

"Watch these hands," he said. "You'll see that they have the true gourmet touch." He reached for a nearby telephone and tapped out a series of numbers that were evidently quite familiar to him. "Pete?" he said, after a momentary pause. "This is Liam Kane. Send over one of your special pizzas with everything on it, will you? Half an hour will be fine." He put down the phone and smiled at her. "If you live in this part of town, who needs to cook?"

Amie took a shower while they waited for the pizza to arrive. She emerged from the guest bathroom to find Liam setting out paper plates on the kitchen table. A very large pizza rested at the center of the table, and Amie needed only one quick look and an even quicker sniff to decide that she was famished.

The pizza disappeared fast. Liam got up with a satisfied sigh and pushed the dirty paper plates and napkins inside the delivery carton. He dropped the package into the garbage bin with a definite flourish. "That's the best part of my gourmet cooking," he said. "No cleaning up afterward. No stacking dishes in the dishwasher and soaking dirty pans." He walked around the table and gently urged Amie to her feet, putting his arm across her shoulders. "See how easy it is?" he said. "I can just put my arm around the woman I'm planning to seduce and lead her into my living room. I switch off the overhead lights, flip the button on my stereo, and there you have it. The perfect setting for a leisurely seduction."

The soft sounds of a Simon and Garfunkel tape filled

the living room, and Amie relaxed against the plump sofa cushions. She wanted Liam to make love to her. There seemed little point in pretending a resistance she didn't feel. His hands caressed her expertly, already knowing her body, knowing how to give her the most exquisite pleasure. She stroked the smooth skin of his back, surrendering herself willingly to the sensuous enchantment of the music and the darkness and Liam.

Even before he lay beside her on the sofa, her stomach was knotted tight with need. She lay back against the cushions, and Liam twisted his hands in the golden strands of her hair, kissing her long and hard. She responded eagerly, welcoming the urgency of his demands. The velvet pillows were warm on her naked back. The heat of Liam's body burned pleasurably against her breast and thighs. Slowly, tenderly, he caressed her until his lovemaking took them beyond simple physical satisfaction to a magic place where for one shimmering, timeless moment they became a single entity, bonded together in their hearts and minds as well as their bodies.

Afterward, they walked together into his bedroom and Amie fell asleep locked in his arms, knowing it was no longer possible to continue lying to him. Tomorrow, whatever the cost, she would have to tell him the truth.

She awoke to find Liam's side of the bed empty and a note pinned to his pillow:

You were sleeping so peacefully, I couldn't bear to disturb you. The executive v.-p. says all hell has broken loose on the Florida project and he needs me in the office. Unless the project manager has been eaten by an alligator, or the problem proves

*similarly intractable, I'll pick you up at your apart-
ment in time for dinner. I love you.*

I love you. The words sang in her ears all the way
back to her apartment. If Liam really loved her, he would
understand how she had been drawn into the terrible mess
of lies and deceptions that had built up between them.
She searched through her closet, decided she had nothing
suitable to wear, and rushed out to buy something. She
chose a full-skirted dress of pale lilac voile trimmed with
white embroidery. It was the sort of soft, feminine cre-
ation she had never worn before, even as a young girl,
but today it suited her mood. When she was near Liam
she felt very much a woman.

By five o'clock she was dressed and waiting, pacing
her small living room and sipping nervously from a glass
of white wine. The sharp sound of her doorbell set off
a flutter of nerves. "Please Lord," she whispered, "let
Liam understand how it all happened."

She pulled open the door, a smile of welcome curving
her lips.

"Well hello, sweetie."

The smile died abruptly. "Jeff," she said tightly. "What
are you doing here? You said you would call on Friday.
This is only Thursday."

"I had a hunch it might be a good idea to check in
with you a little early. When you've spent four years in
jail, you learn to be a bit cautious—and to follow up on
your hunches."

"I'm expecting Liam to arrive at any minute. You'd
better leave, Jeff."

Without bothering to reply, he pushed the door open
and walked past her into the living room. "Nice place
you've made for yourself," he said. "I believe I'll wait

here and you can introduce me to your Mr. Kane. I think I mentioned that I have a friend working in National's accounting department. He needs my help right away if we're going to make a decent profit from all the hard work he's put in already. I want that job in accounts, Amie, and I want you to ask for it tonight."

"Jeff, I already told you. I won't help you get any position where you're handling other people's money."

"I'll wait here," he said, ignoring her refusal. "I'll ask Mr. Kane about the job myself. And if you're smart, you'll keep your mouth shut while I'm asking."

"You can't wait here! Jeff, there's something about Liam Kane you don't know." She swallowed hard, biting back the fear, biting back her impulse to tell him that Liam Kane had once been called Lawrence King. "Liam isn't the sort of man to respond to pressure. I promise you, Jeff, he wouldn't give his own brother a job unless his brother deserved it."

Jeff stood up and grabbed her shoulders. She had forgotten how tall he was until she saw his face looming over hers, his eyes glittering with cruel determination. His mouth finally relaxed into a satisfied smile. "Well, well," he said, "I do believe little Amie has fallen genuinely in love with her boss. You do seem to make a habit of it, don't you, sweetie?"

"No."

His face darkened with an angry flush. "I guess I should congratulate you anyway. It's not bad when a cheap lay like you manages to hook a big fish like Liam Kane, especially since I hear from my friend that he's crazy about you. Sounds like a real touching love story, baby. But you've got to learn to spread your good fortune around a bit. Those innocent baby blue eyes of yours may fool Liam Kane, but I know just what sort of girl you really are. A quick tumble in the sack and you're as ready to compromise your principles as the rest of us. Isn't that right, Amie my sweet?"

She was so angry that she reached up to slap his face without stopping to think. Even a moment's reflection would have warned her that Jeff Cooper was a dangerous man to provoke. He caught her hand easily, twisting it behind her back in a grip that totally prevented her from moving. Her body was thrust tightly against his, and his face hovered over hers, dark with menace.

They both looked up at the sound of footsteps in the hall but Liam walked into the living room before either of them could move. "Amie!" he called out as he came through the doorway. "Your door's not locked; you should be more careful..." His voice died away as he registered the scene in front of him. The evening sun blazed through the apartment windows, highlighting the picture of Amie, apparently locked willingly in Jeff's passionate embrace.

"I'm sorry," he said, his voice sounding cool. "I didn't mean to interrupt anything."

Amie understood in that moment what it must feel like to be a statue. Her limbs seemed to have become solid blocks of heavy marble—far too heavy to move— and for several panic-stricken seconds she couldn't remember how to breathe. It seemed a lifetime before Jeff released his grip on her arms and the power of breathing returned, but she still stood stock still, unable to break out of her physical paralysis. Only her eyes continued to function, registering Liam's appearance with vivid, technicolor clarity.

Jeff turned to greet the newcomer. "Mr. Kane?" he

said, and an easy smile wiped away the previous brutality of his expression. He held out his hand as Liam walked further into the room, and his assured smile suddenly faded. "My God! You're Lawrence King!" He swiveled around furiously to confront Amie. "Why didn't you tell me who he was? Why is he calling himself Liam Kane?"

Amie's paralysis relaxed just enough to enable her to close her eyes. When she opened them again, Liam had walked across the room to stand beside her. He looked somewhat pale; otherwise she could detect no trace of emotion whatsoever on his face. She couldn't understand why he appeared so much in control of himself. Surely he must feel some surprise. Shouldn't there have been a shock of recognition in his eyes when he looked at her and realized for the first time just who she was? She felt his gaze searching her features, and her stomach lurched sickeningly. How could she have forgotten the extent of his self-control? At this moment he looked frighteningly like the Lawrence King who had come four years ago to arrest her. His tawny eyes were expressionless and his face looked hard, remote, as if he were totally incapable of feeling the gentler emotions.

Liam's gaze ran impassively over Jeff's handsome features. "Good evening, Mr. Cooper," he said evenly. "I was told that your request for parole had been approved by the local parole board. How are you?"

Jeff recovered his self-assurance with a speed Amie found amazing. "I guess I'm pretty good, all things considered." He laughed with only a touch of uncertainty. "This is quite like old times, isn't it?" he said. "The three of us all together. You and Amie working for the same company. Has she mentioned to you that I'm hoping to get a job with National?"

Amie's powers of coherent thinking returned sufficiently to make her wonder why Jeff still wanted the job in accounts. Unless by some miracle he'd decided to try to earn a living by honest hard work, what could he possibly hope to gain by pressing Liam for employment? Even he must understand that it would be insane to attempt to defraud National Development when the president of the company knew about his past record.

Liam didn't return Jeff's smile. "No," he said. "Amie's never mentioned your name to me. But I expect she realizes that I don't play favorites. If you want a job with National, Mr. Cooper, our personnel manager will be happy to consider your application without any recommendation from me."

"Yeah, sure he will. And in this economy he's going to hire a man who has no way of explaining where he spent the last four years."

"You could try telling him the truth about where you've been," Liam said evenly. "You might be amazed to find just how far a small dose of honesty will get you."

Jeff's smile was bitter. "Sure. The world's full of bleeding hearts waiting to offer jobs to ex-convicts."

"We have one ex-convict working at National right now, as a matter of fact. I encouraged Mr. Hubert to give this person a chance, and I've been very pleased with the experiment."

"I'll bet you have." Jeff's eyes wandered insultingly in Amie's direction. "Unfortunately, I don't have the physical charms of your other jailbird."

Liam looked consideringly from Amie to Jeff and back again. "If you think I was referring to Ms. Fletcher, you're mistaken," he said. "As far as I am aware, Ms. Fletcher has committed no crime, and she has certainly been convicted of none. The person I spoke of happens to be a man."

"Then you'd be prepared to offer me a job?"

Liam's gaze rested measuringly on Jeff. "That depends," he said, speaking slowly. "I think, however, that it's unlikely. I doubt if we'd agree on what jobs were suitable."

"You're like all the others," Jeff said bitterly. "You're real happy to talk about honesty and hard work, but when it comes right down to it you're never prepared to put your money where your mouth is. You've got your token jailbird working at National, and as far as you're concerned that means the rest of us can be thrown back onto the garbage heap."

Amie's voice returned at last. "Jeff," she said desparately, "please don't. Can't you see this isn't going to get you anywhere?"

"Can't you wait to get rid of me?" Jeff demanded with a sneer. "Are you anxious to turn your charms on Mr. Kane so that he doesn't ask too many awkward questions about what we've been up to these past few weeks?"

"Jeff, please don't do this—"

"Perhaps your Mr. Kane would be grateful to me if I told him a couple of interesting things about you. I'll bet you've fed him a wonderful story about how innocent you were when you worked for West Farm, and how you had no idea what was going on. Well, Mr. Kane, I've got a different version of that sob story of hers. In case you haven't discovered it yet, Amie Fletcher has some mighty expensive tastes and her favors can become a bit costly. She was the one who showed me how we could set up the computer so that there wouldn't be any record of who'd been fixing the books. She was the one who wanted money for clothes and parties and booze and trips overseas. She's an expensive item, Mr. Kane, and I sure hope you have the budget to indulge her taste for luxury."

Amie was shaking with such fury that she could hardly speak. "You're a bastard, Jeff," she said. "And a liar, too." Rage made her stumble over her words. He sounded so horrifyingly convincing. She wrapped her arms protectively around herself and stared down at her shoes. Now that it was all much too late, how she wished she had been courageous enough to tell Liam the truth when she first discovered she loved him. In retrospect it was so easy to see what a fool she'd been!

She could scarcely believe it when she felt Liam's arm drop casually around her shoulders, comforting her and stilling her convulsive shaking. "You're a pretty despicable man, Mr. Cooper," she heard him say. "I'm very well aware of the extent of Amie's involvement in the West Farm fraud case. I was convinced of her innocence four years ago and fought with the district attorney's office to prevent her arrest. I didn't succeed, but believe me, I studied the evidence very carefully and I was convinced then—as I still am today—that Amie should never have even been arrested. As far as I'm concerned, the West Farm fraud case holds only one mystery, which is how a person of Amie's integrity could ever have been deceived by somebody like you, whose basic instincts are so profoundly and lastingly corrupt."

"I can see you've discovered that Amie's a real hot number in bed, Mr. Kane. I guess she's fooled you with the same sort of sweet-sounding pillow talk that had me fooled. She sure does look good lying back on the bed with her hair streaming out over your arm. I can see how

she's got to you, I really can, because that's the exact
same way she got to me. All that ice on the surface and
a furnace underneath. It really turns a man on. You have
my sympathies in advance, Mr. Kane, for the day when
you wake up and see what kind of a woman you've really
got lying next to you."

Liam's hand clenched for a moment on Amie's shoulder, but his voice gave no hint of any emotional dis-
turbance. "I'm content to trust my own judgment," he
said. "I think it's more accurate than yours, Mr. Cooper."

"Then you won't be surprised if I tell you Amie's
been seeing me regularly since I arrived in Chicago, will
you?"

"I think it's time you left," Liam said harshly. "Perhaps *you* won't be surprised if I tell you that I'm aware
of your attempt to plea-bargain four years ago. I know
that you tried to get your own sentence lightened by
promising to implicate Amie. In view of your past behavior toward her, I don't put much faith in your version
of recent events. We have nothing more to discuss, Mr.
Cooper, so perhaps you'd like me to escort you to the
front door."

"I can escort myself," Jeff snarled. He directed a
vicious smile toward Amie. "You've landed a big one,
honey. Make sure you don't blow it before his ring is
on your finger. Remember to open those sapphire-blue
eyes of your real wide if he ever asks any awkward
questions."

Moments later the slam of the front door echoed through
the still living room. Liam's arm dropped from Amie's
shoulders, and he moved away from her to lean against
the small bookcase that stood in a corner of the room.
The silence stretched out while Amie tried to interpret

the taut bleakness of his expression. Finally she managed to find her voice.

"You knew all along about my involvement in the West Farm fraud case," she said. "You already knew who I was. How long ago did you recognize me?"

"My wife died one week before your case came to trial," he said. "How could I ever forget anything about my time in Riverside?"

"I didn't know Liam, I'm so sorry..."

"What for?" he asked with cruel sarcasm. "The fact that Jackie died, or the fact that I recognized your name the moment the personnel manager mentioned it to me?"

"Liam, don't. Please don't be this way." For weeks she had dreaded the moment when he would discover the truth about her past, but in her grimmest imaginings she hadn't adequately visualized the pain that his scorn now provoked. "If you recognized my name, why did you let me apply for the job as your secretary. Why didn't you say something to Mr. Hubert?"

"I didn't say anything because there seemed no reason why I should. Even if you were the Amie Fletcher I knew, you had been convicted of no crime. Why shouldn't you work as my secretary? Besides, I knew there must be hundreds of women with the same name—perhaps thousands. It's not particularly unusual. I wasn't certain who you were until you arrived for the interview."

She fought back a quick gasp of hysterical laughter. So much for all her plans of secret revenge! "You mean to say you recognized me right from the beginning? But I've changed so much."

The bleakness of his expression deepened. "Have you? As I've pointed out to you before, Amie, I'm a professional investigator. I'm trained to look beyond superficial appearances. You've changed your hairstyle, you're fifteen pounds lighter, and you were wearing glasses when I first saw you, but you have the same mannerisms. You have the same soft voice. You have the same smile." Abruptly he turned away and stared out of the window at the summer sun sinking gradually behind the tall apartment buildings. "Damn it, Amie, do you take me for a complete fool? Why do you think I gave you those computer estimates to work on for the Florida project? I always believed Jeff Cooper initiated the fraud at West Farm, but I wanted to see if I were right in thinking you could be trusted around a computer. I'd already made all my own projections, of course. I just wanted to see if your figures tallied with mine."

She started to laugh again, then clamped her lips tightly together. "How fortunate for me that I didn't make any errors."

He continued to stare out the window. "Yes."

She drew in a deep breath, quelling the last remnant of hysteria. "Why didn't you say anything to me, Liam? Why did you let me go on believing you hadn't recognized me?"

"I'm more interested in knowing why *you* didn't say anything to me. Why didn't you ever admit you'd once known me as Lawrence King? I gave you a dozen different opportunities to tell me the truth, but you never took them. What were you setting me up for, Amie? How long have you and Jeff been planning to rip off National Development?"

She realized suddenly that his cool behavior toward Jeff Cooper and his calm explanations to her were nothing more than a front. Beneath his controlled expression and low voice, Liam was seething with white-hot fury. She hurried across the room to his side, clutching at his arm. "Liam, you can't mean that! You must know that I loathe Jeff Cooper. My God, tell me you don't really believe that I'm involved in Jeff's schemes."

He shook her hands away. "So you admit he has schemes that involve National Development. But you didn't tell me about them, did you, Amie? You never came to me and said, 'Liam, I think somebody may be trying to defraud the company.'"

"Jeff only contacted me a couple of days ago. I had nothing to tell you."

"Jeff's been in Chicago for the better part of four weeks. Why else is he hanging around, if not to keep in touch with you?"

"How do you know he's been in Chicago that long?" she asked, realizing too late that her question was bound to create the wrong impression in Liam's mind.

"You should have realized I would be notified by the Department once he was given parole. Lots of people come out of jail with revenge on their minds. Jeff's simply one of many people who'd like to see me come to harm."

"I didn't know he was in town until two days ago. I swear it, Liam."

"Are you suggesting it was his arrival that prompted your frantic decision to skip town? Was your conscience finally bothering you, or were you just afraid of being caught?"

"I was afraid of what Jeff would say to you," she said. "I was afraid of what he'd do to me." She saw the anger that blazed in Liam's eyes, exploding out of the restraints he had put on it. "Liam, you don't understand. I wasn't helping Jeff—"

He slammed his hand on the window ledge. "Damn it, Amie, stop lying to me. There's no need for any more pretending. Do you want the last laugh? Well, here it is. For the past few weeks I've been waiting—hoping—longing—for the moment when you'd show that you'd learned to trust me. I kept thinking that one day you'd tell me the truth without any prompting because you trusted me completely. For a guy who's knocked around the underbelly of the criminal world most of his life, I guess I'm still an idealistic fool. What sort of a sick attraction does Jeff Cooper have for you? Can't you see he's worthless—no, worse than that, vicious?"

"Of course I can," she said tightly. "That's why I was leaving Chicago."

"What a pity I prevented your escape plans by coming to your apartment! We could have saved each other a fair amount of hurt if I'd let you run away when you wanted to. I can only apologize for being so unperceptive about the real state of your feelings. I hope a couple of nights in my bed didn't seem too high a price to pay to keep me from becoming suspicious."

"You know that isn't why I went to bed with you," she said despairingly.

"Wasn't it?" His angry gaze raked her insultingly. "On second thought, you did seem to be having a pretty good time, so I guess I measured up as a lover even if I wasn't quite as easy to rip off as you and Jeff hoped."

Amie stretched out her hand, but he flinched away from the contact and she let it fall back to her side. "Liam, don't hurt us both this way. You don't believe what you're saying, I know you don't. I love you, Liam. You can't truly think I wanted to hurt you. You must know I never planned to deceive you."

He looked at her searchingly. "Didn't you?"

"Of course not." She tried to put all the weight of her love behind the simple statement, but the memory of how she had originally tried to deceive him thickened her words with guilt, and she knew her voice lacked conviction. His mouth twisted into a grim smile and she saw at once that he didn't believe her. Why should he, after all? In a way, his accusations were valid. She was a liar and a cheat, even if she wasn't Jeff's accomplice.

"We both know you're lying, don't we?" he said. She watched in defeated silence as he reached inside his jacket and withdrew a checkbook. He wrote rapidly, his hand slashing across the page as he signed his name.

"Here," he said, ripping the check out and flinging it onto her coffee table. "Here's a month's severance pay in lieu of notice. You'll find I've included a bonus for unpaid overtime in the bedroom. I'd hate you to think all those passionate kisses of yours went unrewarded. Jeff Cooper's right, honey, you're a star performer in the bedroom. If I remember correctly, he paid you with a trip to Jamaica, didn't he? I'm afraid I can't quite match his standards of generosity, but at least I've earned this money, not stolen it. Does that make any difference to you, I wonder."

Even at the trial, Amie had never felt as shocked and humiliated as she did now. "You'd better get out, before I call somebody and have you thrown out," she said. "It must be wonderful to feel so damn sure you're right all the time. As far as I'm concerned, you can take your self-righteousness to bed with you, and I hope it makes a cozy companion!"

Tears were already blinding her eyes, and she didn't wait to see what effect her words had on him. She ran into her bedroom and locked the door behind her. Mo-

ments later, she heard the slam of the front door, and
she pulled her suitcases from the back of the closet. She
was bleeding inside from the wounds Liam had inflicted,
and like any wounded animal she wanted only one thing.
She wanted to go home.

CHAPTER TEN

SOME TIME DURING the endless night she remembered that Jeff Cooper's "friend" was already hard at work in the accounts department, setting up a scheme to defraud National Development. She wrote a brief note to Liam explaining the situation and mailed it to him from the bus station. In the same envelope she enclosed his check, ripped into a dozen tiny pieces.

After dropping the letter into the mailbox, she was aware of almost nothing until the bus driver drew into the narrow parking lot on the outskirts of Riverside. She took a taxi to her parents' home, allowing herself to be driven through the once-familiar streets of the town in a state of suspended animation.

She almost didn't recognize the house. Her parents had painted it since she'd been gone. In her memories it had remained permanently blue with dark wooden shutters, but in reality it shone with a fresh coat of white paint and its spotlessly clean windows sparkled in the sunshine. She paid off the cab and walked slowly up the neat path, put her suitcases down on the front porch, and rang the doorbell. Her hands were damp, although the day wasn't at all humid, and she searched in her purse for a tissue. Her mother seemed to be taking a long time to answer the bell.

At last she heard the sound of a bolt being drawn back—that was another change made during the last four years—and then the door was opened and her mother was there, as thin and neat as ever. "H–hello, Mother," Amie said. "H–how are you?"

"*Amie?* Amie, is that really you? You've changed your hair and lost weight."

"Yes."

Her mother had never been a woman to dramatize her feelings, and the brief stirring of deep emotion quickly vanished from her eyes. She smoothed a nonexistent crease in her green apron. "Well, come inside, don't hang about. If you arrived on the afternoon bus, you must be thirsty."

Amie picked up her suitcases and carried them into the narrow hallway. "Leave them there," her mother said. "We can take them upstairs later. Go into the living room, why don't you, and I'll fix us a glass of iced tea."

"Can I help?"

"No, the tea is already cooling in the fridge. You sit down and make yourself at home." The incongruity of the remark seemed to strike both of them at once, and Amie smiled nervously as her mother retreated toward the kitchen. "I'll be right back," Mrs. Fletcher said.

Amie stood awkwardly in the middle of the living room. Only important visitors were ever taken there, and she felt ill at ease in its gleaming overfurnished formality. She sat down on one of the stuffed velour chairs, then jumped up and hurried toward the kitchen. She quietly pushed open the door.

Her mother was standing at the big old-fashioned sink, tears trickling silently down her cheeks. As soon as she caught sight of Amie, she turned away and ripped a paper towel off the roll, scrubbing at her tears. "I'm bringing the tea right out," she said. "I was just slicing up some lemon."

Amie hesitated on the threshold of the kitchen, appalled by her mother's grief. She had never seen her cry before. "Mother," she said, "please tell me what's wrong. Is there some way I can help? If there is, please tell me."

Her mother's face remained averted. "I thought you were never going to come home," she said, her voice muffled by the paper towel. "Oh, Amie, we've missed you so, your Dad and I."

A strange, hot ache began to grow in Amie's throat. "You've missed me?" she said. "But you and Dad wanted me to leave Riverside! You told me I should go to Chicago." She swallowed hard, trying to diminish the lump of unshed tears. "I thought . . . I thought you were ashamed of me because of what happened with Jeff Cooper and West Farm Insurance."

Her mother turned around, astonishment drying the last of her tears. "We weren't ashamed of you," she said. "How could you think such a thing? We just wanted you to have a chance to start over, to get your confidence back by holding down a good job in a big city."

"Whenever I called you and Dad at Christmas or on

your birthdays, you always sounded so uncomfortable, as if you wished you weren't talking to me."

Her mother's cheeks darkened with an uncomfortable flush of color. "Well, we never quite knew what to say to you. Your father and I aren't much good at talking about the way we feel, especially on a long-distance phone call. We were both born during the Depression, and I guess our parents were too busy feeding us and seeing that we had shoes on our feet to have time to spare for saying how much they loved us. Your Dad and I, we grew up thinking love was something you showed, not something you talked about."

"When I was arrested, it seemed as though I'd ruined all your dreams for my future," Amie said huskily. "I didn't think you could possibly still love me."

"Oh, Amie, that's not true. You were young and there's no denying you made some bad decisions, but your father and I have always been proud of you. How could we help it? An A student, the prettiest girl in town... And as for loving you—if our parents only loved us when we behaved sensibly, I think most of us would be mighty short of love."

"Then why were you and Dad so eager to get me out of town? I don't understand..."

"We thought *you* wanted to leave! When we saw you in the courtroom during your trial, we could tell how much you hated all the gossip. We thought you'd prefer a fresh start in a bigger town, someplace where there would be room to breathe without the neighbors feeling entitled to report back on it. Besides, quite apart from what happened with Jeff Cooper and the insurance agency, there's not much opportunity for a girl with your training in a tiny place like Riverside."

"If only I'd known how you really felt!" She swallowed hard. "I've been so afraid to come home, so afraid to face you both."

"We never knew you wanted to come back to Riverside. You always sounded as if you were having such a wonderful time in Chicago that we didn't want to press you to come back."

"And all the time I was longing for you to invite me home! Oh, Mom, why didn't we ever tell each other what we really thought? Why did we each expect the other person to be a long-distance mind reader?"

"I don't know. But sometimes, when I can't find the right words to say something, I just don't say anything at all. Like I said, it was the way we were brought up to behave."

Amie looked at her mother's wiry, work-hardened body and felt her throat constrict with emotion. She reached out tentatively and grasped her mother's hand. "Mom, thank you," she said. "You've made me understand something about myself that I never fully realized before. I'm more like you and Dad than I ever suspected. I don't know how to talk about my feelings either, and when I get too confused, when too many conflicting emotions are all piled up inside me, I just run away. I'm twenty-six years old, and I'm only just learning how to confront a problem head-on."

Mrs. Fletcher seemed to need something to do with her hands, so she began slicing another lemon into the tea. "I'm not sure a bit of reticence is all that bad. There're people who come on television and tell the whole world more about their feelings than I've ever told any single person about mine." She turned on the cold water and rinsed the lemon juice off her fingertips. "On the other hand, who knows? Maybe those people on TV are right after all. My mother drummed it into me that respectable folk keep their troubles to themselves; but perhaps if she'd confided in somebody occasionally, she wouldn't have dropped dead of exhaustion before she was fifty."

Amie forced herself to meet her mother's eyes. She cleared her throat pushing the words out. "I was running away from a personal problem when I came home today," she said. She got up from her chair and began to pace around the kitchen. "I've fallen in love, Mom, and this time it's real—the kind that only happens once in a lifetime, the kind that tears you apart if something goes wrong. We had some misunderstanding—it's a long story—but I ran away because I didn't have the courage to tell Liam the truth about the way I feel. I was too much of a coward to stay and fight for what I wanted, so I ran away before he could hurt me. Listening to you, thinking about what a mess I've made of my relationship with you and Dad over the last four years, I've realized that I can't let the same thing happen with Liam. Heaven knows, I ought to have learned by now that however far you run, your problems come right along with you. The last four years in Chicago have taught me that much."

"Liam," said her mother, as if testing the word on her tongue. "What's his other name?"

"Kane. His name's Liam Kane."

Her mother's smile held an unexpected touch of wryness. "Until today, I never actually saw a girl who looked lovesick just saying a man's name. Well, am I right in thinking you won't be staying with us very long? I have the feeling you're planning to turn right around and go back to this Liam on tonight's bus. Am I right?"

Amie smiled back at her mother. Her body suddenly felt light and full of energy. "I'll stay in Riverside over the weekend," she said. "I'd like to help Dad in the hardware store tomorrow, and I sure don't want to miss out on one of your Sunday dinners. I've almost forgotten what roasted chicken and home-baked biscuits taste like." She bent and dropped a quick, hesitant kiss on her mother's cheek, smelling the once-familiar scent of soap and talcum powder and baking spices that clung to her mother's skin. "Oh, Mom, it's good to be home!"

Mrs. Fletcher searched in the pocket of her apron and retrieved a large white handkerchief. She blew her nose and reached for the jug of iced tea. "We may as well sit in here while we drink this," she said, drawing a chair up to the scrubbed wooden table. "There's no point carrying this heavy tray into the living room."

"Mmm. It's nicer in here anyway."

"Bring that Liam home to meet us," her mother said, giving her glass of iced tea a vigorous, unnecessary stir. "And don't wait another four years before you do it. Are those words clear enough for you?"

"They're clear enough." Amie smiled shyly, unable to believe that she was actually sharing this moment of intimacy with her mother. "I'm not deaf, you know, Mom. Just a bit of a slow learner."

Her father drove her into Springfield late Sunday afternoon, and she caught the evening bus back to Chicago. She was tempted to go straight from the terminal to Liam's apartment, but she felt travel-worn and rumpled, so she returned to Evanston and showered quickly, changing into sapphire-blue cotton pants and a white open-weave shirt. Glancing at herself in the mirror before she left for his apartment, she felt a fleeting moment of astonishment that she, Amie Fletcher, was actually the sensuous, vibrantly alive woman reflected there.

But when she gave her name to the security guard at Liam's apartment building, she felt jittery and ill at ease. What if he had some woman in his apartment? What if he refused to see her? Why wasn't he answering his buzzer?

Liam finally answered the intercom, putting an end to her spiraling state of nerves. "Ms. Fletcher is here to see you," the doorman said. "She says you might be expecting her, or you might not." His tone of voice implied that in a well-ordered world, people were either expected or they weren't. He looked disapprovingly at Amie over his narrow spectacles while they both waited for Liam's reply.

There was a long pause, during which she could hear only the crackle of static on the intercom. "Send her up," Liam said, and abruptly broke the connection.

"Mr. Kane's apartment is on the penthouse floor," the doorman informed her.

"I know where he lives," she said. "Thank you."

Liam was waiting for her when she got out of the elevator. His door was open and he was leaning against the frame, a drink in his hand. His dark hair gleamed in the reflected glow of the bright hall light, but his tawny eyes seemed shuttered and opaque, sealing in all his thoughts and emotions.

Amie had worked out the exact words she was going to say when she saw him again, but now every syllable flew from her mind and she stood mute on his doorstep, waiting to see what he would do. After a moment's silence, the shuttered look disappeared from his eyes. He reached out and touched her cheek. "Hi," he said, "Welcome home."

She was tempted to throw herself into his arms and forget about explanations, but she was determined that for once she was going to put everything she was feeling into words so that there would be no possible room left for misunderstanding. "May I come in?" she asked finally. "I'd like to explain some things to you, if I can."

He stood aside as she walked into the living room. "Would you like a drink?" he asked.

She shook her head. "I've come to explain about Jeff," she said. "I can't bear to have you think I was helping him defraud the company."

"I know you weren't," he said quietly. "Amie, before you say anything more, I have some apologizing to do." He ran his fingers through his hair in a quick, nervous gesture. "I behaved like a jealous fool Thursday night. I accused you of crimes I knew you hadn't committed because I was hurt and angry and I didn't know how to cope with my own feelings. I'd been waiting so long to have you tell me the truth about yourself. I tried every way I knew to get you to confide in me, but you never would. Seeing Jeff Cooper in your apartment, listening to his poisonous lies, I felt for one black moment that you must have been deliberately deceiving me. I couldn't handle that possibility, Amie, and I exploded."

"You seemed pretty much under control to me."

"I'm good at concealing the truth about my feelings— my work as an investigator required it. Frankly, I think we'd all have been better off if I'd just done what I felt like doing, and to hell with the consequences."

"What did you want to do?"

"Punch Jeff Cooper on the nose and take you to bed. Not necessarily in that order."

She smiled wryly. "I think your basic instincts were sound."

There was a moment's pause. "Amie," he said, staring into his drink, "why didn't you ask for my help when Cooper tried to blackmail you?"

"I wanted to tell you the truth so many times," she said, "but I was too scared. I was so afraid you would despise me."

"*Despise you!* Damn it, Amie, I'm in love with you! What in the world have I ever done to make you think I could possibly despise you?"

She laughed then, a tight, nervous laugh. "Have you seen a videotape of yourself in court, Liam? Have you ever imagined how utterly ruthless, how *arrogantly* incorruptible you look to somebody on the witness stand? I was a young, frightened girl when I was arrested, and the memory of your behavior in court haunted my nightmares for years. Whatever your opinion of me is today, I know that at the time of my trial you thought I was guilty. Is it surprising that I was afraid to confide in you? Try to see things from my point of view, Liam."

He could not have appeared more stunned by her words if she'd accused him of attempted murder. "What in the name of God are you talking about? I thought you were innocent from the first moment I arrived in Riverside. I fought in every way I knew to keep the government from pursuing its case against you. But in view of Jeff Cooper's explicit testimony, there was nothing I could do." His mouth drew into a grim line. "Everything I said in that courtroom was carefully calculated to persuade the jury of your innocence."

you love me." The last words were no more than a murmur against her mouth as his lips covered hers in a passionate kiss. She felt the quick shudder of his body as
she responded to his touch, twining her fingers in the
thickness of his hair. Without another word, he picked
her up and carried her into the bedroom, and she clung
to him as if she never wanted to let him go. He laid her
gently on the bed, but as she moved to pull him down
beside her, her legs encountered a canvas bag.

"Liam?" she said. "There's a suitcase on your bed."

Even in the semi-darkness she saw the brief gleam of
humor in his eyes. "I was packing when you arrived,"
he acknowledged. "Whether or not you loved me, I wasn't
prepared to let you walk out of my life without a struggle.
I had to wait in Chicago until the indictment against the
accountant went through or I'd have been beating on
your parents' front door yesterday afternoon."

"Very cavemanish," she said huskily. "What were you
planning to do with me? Sling me over your shoulder
and hide me away at the back of your den?"

"I'll show you what I was planning to do," he said.
He tossed the bag onto the floor and began to undress.
His fingers were shaking as he fumbled with the buttons
of his shirt, and a hot flush of desire burned her skin as
the sexual tension stretched tauter and tauter between
them. When he was naked, he sat on the edge of the bed
and she slowly pulled off her blouse and unzipped her
sapphire-blue pants, knowing that his fever-bright gaze
was following every movement. When she had taken off
all her clothes, she reached out her arms and he came
into them, kissing her as if he were starving for the taste
of her.

She met his hunger with an answering hunger of her

own. Her hands clung to his shoulders, and she writhed beneath him on the bed as he took possession of her body. "I love you, Liam," she whispered, and as if the words were a signal, her world exploded, fusing their bodies into one blazing, perfect whole.

They lay there for a long time, tangled in each other's arms, and he kissed her tenderly. "Amie," he said, "I love you so much. Will you marry me?"

She curled more closely against his body and smoothed an unruly strand of hair away from his forehead. She was so replete with love that she could hardly find the words to answer him. She brushed a fingertip down the side of his cheek. "Marry you?" she repeated wonderingly. "You want to marry me?"

"Yes," he said. "Tomorrow morning, or maybe the next day if we have to wait that long to get a license."

"Would you settle for next Saturday?" she asked. "My parents would be thrilled if we had the ceremony in their local church and the minister only marries people on Saturdays."

"I guess I could handle a five-day delay," he said. "Come to think of it, my mother would be pleased. If the wedding isn't until next weekend, it would give her time to join us."

"You have a mother?" Amie exclaimed drowsily, her mind still drugged by Liam's lovemaking. "I never realized you had a mother."

He laughed, then nuzzled her ear. "That must have been some performance I just gave in bed! Honey, I'm sorry to disillusion you, but not only do I have a mother, I also have it on the best authority that I arrived in this world exactly the same way as everybody else."

She wriggled provocatively against him. "How boring! And I thought at the very least you'd been sent to earth in a sealed space capsule. You know, a gift to the planet Earth—and especially to me—from a faraway galaxy."

His hand curved gently around her breast. "Did I ever mention that you talk a great deal of nonsense?"

She touched her fingers to his lips. "Who's talking?" she murmured.

"Not me," he said. His mouth trailed kisses down her throat and his hands roamed over her body, bringing magic in the wake of their touch.

She knew that some devastatingly witty remark hovered on the tip of her tongue, just waiting to be spoken. She opened her mouth. "I love you," she said.

"I love you too," Liam replied softly and her witty remark, whatever it might have been, was lost forever in the passion of his kiss.

All of the above titles are $1.75 per copy

Available at your local bookstore or return this form to:

SECOND CHANCE AT LOVE
Book Mailing Service
P.O. Box 690, Rockville Centre, NY 11571

Please send me the titles checked above. I enclose _____
Include $1.00 for postage and handling if one book is ordered; 50¢ per book for
two or more. California, Illinois, New York and Tennessee residents please add
sales tax.

NAME _____

ADDRESS _____

CITY _____ STATE/ZIP _____
(allow six weeks for delivery)   SK-41